'I really like adventure stories like this. I couldn't wait to see what happened next. I always thought there might be pirates on Portland.'

(James aged 8)

'Carol has the knack of bringing to life the local myths of the island, in such a way that a girl of 66 can enjoy the fantasy of it all. In this story, Suzie even shares my enthusiasm for cats!'

(Barbara aged 66)

'I love spotting the real place names in Portland Pirates. Now I want to go to Portland Bill and look for the mermaid.'

(Madelaine aged 9)

'I like it that it's kind of a ghostly pirate ship and crew from the past, but they're also real, raiding the shops and eating baked beans. The chapter endings are good cliffhangers, you wonder what's going to happen next.'

(William aged 11)

Also available in

THE PORTLAND CHRONICLES

The Portland Sea Dragon

Enchantment of the Black Dog

Coming soon

The Portland Giant

Roving
Press

Visit www.rovingpress.co.uk

THE PORTLAND CHRONICLES

PORTLAND
PIRATES

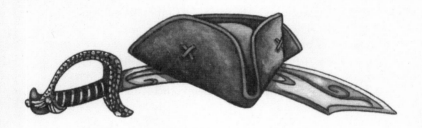

CAROL HUNT

ROVING PRESS

Published by Roving Press Ltd
4 Southover Cottages, Frampton, Dorset, DT2 9NQ, UK
Tel: +44 (0)1300 321531
www.rovingpress.co.uk

First published 2011 by Roving Press Ltd
ISBN: 978-1-906651-11-4

British Library Cataloguing in Publication Data
A catalogue record for this book is available from the British
Library

Illustrations and cover artwork by Domini Deane

Set in Minion 11/13.5 pt by www.beamreachuk.co.uk
Printed and bound in Poland by www.polskabook.co.uk

THE DREAM

Isabel Maydew clung to the main mast of a ship. Giant waves were surging from the west, forcing the ship towards rocks that jutted from the sea. The Isle of Portland loomed ahead like a gloomy whale. Tugging her hood over her face, Isabel edged cautiously along the rigging as the wind howled above her.

A wave like the tail of a giant fish crashed over the ship, knocking her off her feet and washing her towards the bow. She slid along the deck, her arms raised against the rain. A boy flung out his arm and caught her. He pulled her towards a mermaid figurehead, which gazed coldly over the churning waves. Isabel grasped the mermaid's tail with slippery hands. The boy pointed ahead of them, towards the spectre of the lighthouse.

'The Beal o' Portland!' he shouted into the wind. 'Red Pete says we're in grave danger, that the Siren sent this storm to punish 'im. We 'ave to reach the east coast afore she destroys the *Fortune*!'

Brushing rainwater from her eyes, Isabel looked at the man at the ship's helm, steering the ship through the perilous seas. His long coat flapped around him as he fought to keep the ship afloat. The *Fortune's* wheel spun in his hands and the boat lurched sideways. A beam of yellow light from the lighthouse shone over the waves and Isabel suddenly glimpsed a silver flash in the water. 'The mermaid!' she cried.

'Who *are* you?' The boy pushed the hood back from her face and stared at her. The ship tipped again and the boy stumbled. He slipped away from her, tumbling over and over until a wave caught him and swept him into the sea.

Shivering, Isabel awoke from her dream to the sound of skylarks singing over the towering west cliffs of Portland near her home in Weston. The morning sun was shining through the bedroom window, promising another fine July day.

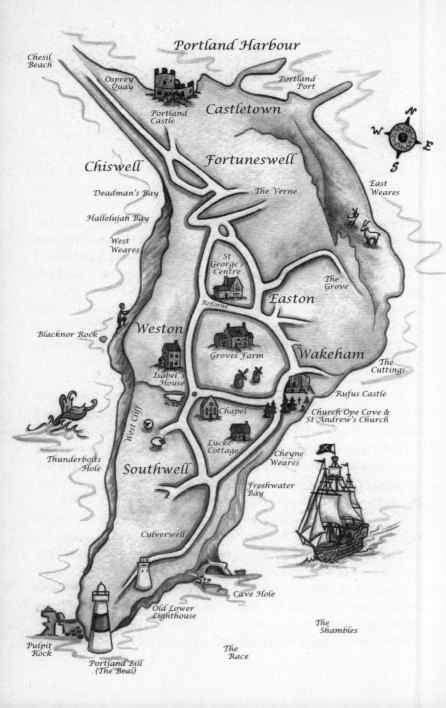

CHAPTER ONE

SEEKING THE *FORTUNE*

Miranda Greychurch sneaked out from the chapel that stood between Smugglers' Cottage and Quarry View House. She ran across the sunlit dusty road. A scruffy black and white sheepdog, Gregor from Groves Farm, ran by her side. After lurking in Weston for nearly an hour, she was heading for the bus stop, where she had finally spotted Isabel Maydew.

Isabel sighed, 'Oh no, it's Miranda.'

'Not her again!' said Ben Lau, Isabel's friend. 'She gives me the creeps.' He tugged his long black fringe over his eyes and plugged in his earphones to listen to music.

Isabel's 5-year-old sister Suzie agreed, 'She's scary.'

'Aachoo!' Snuffling with hay fever, Miranda shoved a lead into Isabel's hand. Gregor gazed up at her with round brown eyes. 'I can't look after Gregor today; you'll have to take him. He keeps eating everything, even yucky stuff. You're used to dealing with animals,' Miranda insisted, looking down her nose at Suzie, who was wearing a swimsuit and black pirate hat crammed over her messy fair hair. Suzie clutched a fishing net in one hand, and with the other she stuffed a melting ice cream on Gregor's nose. He gobbled it up in two bites, spraying slobber over Miranda.

'Yuck!' said Miranda. She wiped the end of her pink nose on a soggy tissue. 'I hate the summer.'

Gregor bounced around Suzie, his tongue lolling from his mouth, his fluffy tail wagging. She leaned over and hugged him until he squeaked.

'But we're going to the rock pools at Portland Bill. It's *your* turn to have Gregor today,' said Isabel.

Miranda shook her head, noting the untidy freckles on Isabel's nose. 'Nope. I'm meeting friends in Weymouth. Unlike you, I have *cool* friends. Are you going rock climbing? I'll listen to the radio later, in case they mention an accident.' She ran her fingers through her long fair hair. Isabel felt her cheeks glowing bright pink.

'Wha' did she say?' asked Ben, removing one earphone.

'I said, where's your friend Wolven today?' Miranda shouted at him.

'He's away at a windsurfing competition,' said Ben nervously.

Miranda sniffed. 'I always thought he was weird, like you.'

'She's scary!' squawked a voice above them. Startled, they all looked up at a green and yellow budgerigar, hopping along the bus sign. The budgie watched them with black beady eyes set in chubby yellow cheeks. It smoothed the feathers of its glossy green chest and whistled before flapping away.

'I hate birds,' said Miranda.

Ben looked thoughtful. 'Budgies don't generally live wild in Dorset.'

Suzie hugged Gregor again, burying her face in his fur. 'Pooh,' she said. 'He smells.'

'Stick him in the sea. He'll smell better after a swim, and so will you and your sister.' Miranda swanned off, swinging a large flowery bag bulging with bikinis and sun cream.

'Rude girl!' shouted Suzie after her. 'When I grow up I'm gonna be a pirate an' I'll fight you with my sword!'

Isabel looked down at Gregor and sighed. She had already offered to look after him for Mrs Groves, his owner, the following day. Gregor panted up at her and shook out his fur until it stood out around him like a black and white powderpuff.

'Poor Gregor, he's hot, the sea'll cool him down,' suggested Suzie.

'I think we should take him with us. The bus is here anyway,' said Ben.

They found seats on the open-top bus, which rambled south by the fields of Weston towards Avalanche Church. Gregor jumped up beside Isabel, and Suzie squashed onto the edge of the seat. 'Budge up,' she said. Ben sat behind them. They passed the small church and travelled through the village of Southwell, where stone cottages clustered by the road and swallows swooped like tiny arrows in the sky. Turning into the long winding road to Portland Bill, the red and white lighthouse appeared like a stripy stick of rock on the edge of sparkling July seas. The bus veered around a corner and Gregor landed on Isabel. The wind streamed through his fur and he smelled of old rug. He thrust his nose over Isabel's shoulder to get a better view, his paws scrabbling on her legs.

'Gerroff, Gregor,' Isabel huffed, pushing him back on to his seat.

Suzie took off her hat and pulled a notepad out from the brim. 'I'm making notes for my *Maydew's Moggies* webpage. "Groover's a big ole cat but very friendly. Nellie's a black cat and could be trained to do magic. Surfer's fluffy and likes food an' fuss",' she read aloud. She chewed the rubber at the end of the pencil. Suzie was keeping three cats in baskets in the kitchen at home, strays found wandering the island. Her mother had agreed to her keeping them until the local animal rescue centre could find suitable homes.

'Look at that cloud. It's a pirate ship!' she shrieked, leaning across Isabel and Gregor.

Isabel stared at the sky, where a swirling white cloud sailed above the ocean. For a moment she saw billowing sails and rows of cannon. Below the cloud ship, currents clashed in the Portland *Race* sending white froth surging across the water.

'It was just a cloud, Suzie,' she said uneasily. She scanned the coast until her eyes ached. Night after night she dreamed of a ship called the *Fortune* sailing to Portland in a ferocious storm. When she closed her eyes, she saw the cabin boy falling into the sea and the white arms of her old enemy, the Portland mermaid.

'I'm gonna have a pirate ship when I'm big,' said Suzie, 'wiv pieces of eight and my own special parrot.' She stuffed her pirate hat back on her head.

'How long has Suzie been a pirate?' asked Ben.

'About 3 weeks,' said Isabel, 'since she read a pop-up book called *Pandora, the Portland Pirate*.'

The bus swayed past the Old Lower Lighthouse, the narrow road twisting through fields of grass dotted with golden flowers. Sunlight glittered like diamonds on the choppy sea surrounding Portland Bill. The air was heavy and hot.

'We're here! Let's pretend we're pirates an' catch us some fishies,' squeaked Suzie, pushing her way to the steps.

'I wouldn't want to meet a *real* pirate,' said Ben, as he followed Suzie, jumping from the bus.

Suzie dashed ahead. As they walked past the old red crane towards the rock pools of the south-east coast, a heat haze rose from the sea like a host of shimmering ghosts. Purple clouds lined the distant sandy cliffs of the mainland.

Gregor tugged her along the track, his head down, gasping with excitement. Beside the path, waves crashed on the rocks and a sudden breeze blew away Suzie's hat. A distant voice roared, 'Lower the sails!'

'I'll take Gregor,' announced Suzie, chasing her hat. 'I'm training 'im as my pirate dog. We're gonna catch a big mackerel fishy. We can cook 'im over a fire.' She snatched the lead from Isabel.

'You're not making a fire,' said Isabel firmly.

She trailed her eyes along the waves, crashing just below them on the rocks. She saw something move out of the corner of her eye, a tail flicking in the water, and heard voices again.

'Did you hear that?'

'What?' asked Ben. He was looking at the plants that grew around the colourful beach huts near the old lighthouse. Red Admiral butterflies fluttered from leaf to leaf.

'Someone shouted.'

Suzie rested a hand on Isabel's arm. 'Are ye havin' a funny 10 minutes, me heartie?' she asked. 'I 'spect you're heels over head cos it's your birthday soon and you're gonna be 13.'

'Just a week away. I can't wait to see the cake!' said Ben. 'Catch you both later. I'm going to look for puffins by Pulpit Rock.'

'See you,' said Isabel. 'I'll walk up by Cave Hole.' The ancient lair of the phantom Black Dog of Portland always fascinated her.

'*I* can make a fire, we'll cook a fishy,' whispered Suzie to Gregor, as she splashed into the rock pools with the dog at her heels. Gregor sniffed loudly among the seaweed for tiny crabs.

'Don't go far,' warned Isabel. 'I don't want to have to call the Coastguard again.'

'Gregor and me was playin' hide-'n'-seek.'

'They found you at Weymouth Pavilion, 9 miles away!' yelled Isabel.

'We hid on one of them coaches in the lighthouse car park,' smiled Suzie. 'Then it drove off.' She ruffled Gregor's ears. 'It was great! The ladies on the coach were singing *A Life on the Ocean Wave.*' She waded deeper into a rock pool and looked at a red anemone. She poked it with her finger, watching the tiny tendrils open and close.

Isabel climbed to a ledge above Cave Hole and peered into the dark cavern, almost expecting to see the green eyes of a phantom Black Dog staring back at her. She left the spooky cave to climb across the sunlit rocks and dangle her feet in the cool sea. She gazed up at a sky as blue and fragile as a cornflower. Seagulls glided in circles above her. She scanned the shores of the Dorset mainland, where smugglers once sailed along the Jurassic coast by the villages of Osmington and Ringstead. A gentle breeze from the north puffed across the water, sending breaths of soft darkness rippling from Weymouth Bay. She thought about the *Fortune*, the ship of her dreams, and wondered what it would be like to set sail on a ship with towering masts and white sails, with a mermaid figurehead at the bow.

'I would sail around Portland, by Church Ope and alongside the currents at the Bill, then down the west coast,' she daydreamed aloud, pushing her curling brown hair away from her eyes. She imagined herself standing on a warm deck as the sails rippled in the summer breeze.

A soft white mist swirled up from the sea and drifted towards her. The mist touched her lightly like ghostly fingers, leaving her shivering. Suddenly a white hand lunged from the water and twined itself around her ankle. Isabel shrieked.

'Ssister, are you sseeking the *Fortune*?' said a cold voice.

'Let go!' cried Isabel.

The mermaid gripped Isabel's leg tightly. Her red hair swirled around her like eels. With a flick of her strong wrist, the mermaid flipped Isabel into a somersault. She crashed into the sea, her arms flailing, legs kicking. The mermaid surged to her side, seized her hair and smiled menacingly. Her eyes were flecked deep green and blue, like the sea. She tossed tangled red hair away from her thin face, and laughed at her prey.

'Poor Issabel Maydew, looking for a pirate sship.'

'A *pirate* ship!' gasped Isabel. 'Ow! Let go of my hair.' She trod water and tried to unhook the mermaid's fingers. 'Are you spying on me?'

'Of course,' said the mermaid. 'Your ancestor Agness Maydew wass the island witch. She summoned creatures from the depthss of the ssea. She knew the secretss of time. Now *you* are calling the pirates from the passt.'

'I'm not calling pirates! Leave me alone!' shouted Isabel, trying to free herself.

'Come with me.'

The mermaid gripped her arm and dived beneath the waves, pulling Isabel down to the underwater caverns, deeper and deeper. Isabel knew it was useless to struggle. She let the mermaid guide her, curious to see what was lurking so far beneath the waves. A group of dark green sea turtles swam by. She glimpsed a lobster lurking in a rocky crevice on the sea bed, by the shattered masts and splintered keel of an old shipwreck. She saw rows of dark iron cannon and tumbled chests and barrels. Her lungs bursting, she managed to free herself from the mermaid's grip. Icy fingers clutched at her, but she kicked her legs frantically and reached the surface, gasping for air. The mermaid appeared beside her, her eyes as cold as marbles. She flipped her tail, flicking salt water into Isabel's face.

'You've called a pirate captain and his cabin boy across time!' She seized Isabel with her cold hands. 'The *Fortune* belongs here on the sea bed. It'ss mine by right. Red Pete defied me.'

A red fishing boat chugged nearby, bobbing over the waves.

The mermaid released her. 'Sswim free. For now. One day you'll share all your ssecrets with me.' With a cold smile and a final flick of her turquoise tail, the mermaid vanished beneath the waves.

'I dreamt about a ship and a cabin boy! They can't be real!' gulped Isabel.

She felt the burning marks of the mermaid's fingers on her arms, like jellyfish stings, as she swam towards the shore, the waves lifting and dropping her in the gentle swell. The treacherous mermaid, a creature as ancient as the lost island of Atlantis, always seemed to be several flips of her tail ahead of Isabel. They had become enemies when she travelled across time to solve two island mysteries, setting free a lonely Sea Dragon and discovering the true identity of the Black Dog.

'Surely the *Fortune*'s just a dream?' she wondered again.

A thin arm reached from the sea ahead of her and disappeared again. Isabel trod water. A boy spluttered, his arms splashing, struggling to stay afloat in the waves swirling around the rocks. Isabel swam to his side. He clutched her shoulder.

'The mermaid left me in the sea, I had to swim for shore,' he gasped.

'Oh no,' said Isabel, recognising the cabin boy from the *Fortune*. 'This can't be happening!'

CHAPTER TWO

A PIRATE CRIME WAVE

Mrs Veronica Greychurch stepped outside her Portland Bill beach hut, which she had decorated with flowery wallpaper and neat blue curtains. She threw a tablecloth over the outdoor table and lined up a shiny fork and knife. She swept back her white blonde hair and straightened the pleated skirt that ended by her chubby knees. On the table she arranged a heap of books. *A General History of Pirates* teetered on top. A child trotted by with a fishing net, tugging Gregor behind her. It was that awful Suzie Maydew in a swimsuit and ridiculous pirate hat. Mrs Greychurch shuddered. She liked to keep a close eye on the Maydews. Suzie's sister Isabel was always in trouble, unlike her own dear daughter Miranda.

Mrs Greychurch peered across the sea. She had chosen this beach hut for its views of the English Channel, stretching towards the Isle of Wight to the east and France to the south. There were pirates, vagabonds, plying their evil trade out there on the sea. Mrs Greychurch was all that stood between the island and a tidal wave of pirates, surging over them and sweeping away decent people.

She cut her cucumber sandwiches into neat squares and wiped the kitchen surfaces with lemon-fresh cleaner. Then she swept the floor again. With a final quick dust of the picture of Blackbeard, a notorious pirate with a bushy black beard, she put her plate on a tray and sat down to enjoy her lunch in peace. She perched sunglasses on her nose to read the *Dorset Echo*.

'Pirate Crime Wave Shocks Portland,' she read aloud. 'In scenes of shocking horror, a Plymouth merchant boat was attacked yesterday by a pirate ship, the *Fortune*. Food and other goods were taken by a swashbuckling captain calling himself Red Pete, who threatened the crew with a sword. One of the terrified crew told our reporter, "He wore a proper pirate hat and was armed to the teeth. I've never seen anything like it."'

Mrs Greychurch tutted. 'A sword *and* teeth – terrible! And to think he's still out there.' Thank goodness she had this beach hut as a look-out. She was going to have to be extra watchful.

The boy staggered across the rocks and fell to his knees, water dripping from his clothes. Isabel looked down at him, catching her breath. His trousers were ripped at the knees, his shirt torn. He pushed tangled copper-coloured hair from his eyes. Freckles were scattered across his nose and pale cheeks.

'How did you end up in the sea?' she asked.

'The *Fortune* was caught in a storm. Red Pete took the helm to sail us roun' the Beal.' He pointed at her, his hand shaking. 'I remember a stowaway. She looked like you.'

Isabel crouched beside the boy from her dream. She guessed he was about 13 years old, the same age as her though not as tall as she was. His arms and legs were thin. She studied his clothes, the coarse cloth of his shirt, the small pearly buttons. On the boy's forearm was a black tattoo of a ship's wheel. He pulled down his sleeve, feeling her eyes on him, shivering. 'Thought I was dead, for sure,' he added. 'Where am I?'

'You're on the Isle of Portland in Dorset.'

The boy nodded, relieved. 'O' course. We were sailing to the Weares south of Church Ope. That's where the ship'll be anchored. Take more 'n a wave or two to sink the *Fortune*. She's a sturdy ship.' The boy looked at Isabel with curious dark brown eyes. 'T'was a terrible storm an' bad luck to find a stowaway aboard.'

He studied her for a minute, then held out his hand. 'P'raps I was mistaken. My name's Tom Lucke.'

'Hello, I'm Isabel,' she said, shaking his cold hand. 'Is it true the *Fortune*'s a pirate ship?'

'O' course. The *Fortune* is Red Pete's ship,' said the boy, 'a pirate cap'n. Everyone fears 'im. They say he's like Harry Paye, that famous Poole pirate o' years ago. Red Pete's stolen more gold from the Spaniards than any other pirate.'

The sea lapped the rocks beside them, the water glooping, leaving circles of white froth.

'And you're called Tom *Lucke*,' Isabel said thoughtfully. 'Lucke's a Portland name.'

Tom nodded. 'I live in Weston with me cousin Beth at Lucke Cottage.' He shook sea water from his clothes, already drying in the bright sunshine, and looked around. 'I s'pose I'll 'ave to go back to the ship an' fetch 'n' carry from dawn till dusk for them pirates.'

Isabel interrupted, 'There's something you should know. What date d'you *think* it is?'

'Reckon it's Tuesday, July 24th. Me birthday's a week away, the 31st. I'll be 13 years of age.'

'Me too!' said Isabel, surprised. 'We have the same birthday. But d'you remember the year?'

'1691, o' course.'

Before Isabel could explain any further, she was pushed aside.

'Where've ye been, young varmint?' demanded a pirate with a blue scarf wrapped around his head. He wore a tight black waistcoat and his scrawny legs poked from tattered trousers. His watery eyes were set wide apart above a beaky nose, like a parrot. He jumped across the rocks to Tom, gripped him by the scruff of his shirt and hauled him to his feet.

'Cutlass!' gasped the boy.

'Shorty and Bill 'ave been hollerin' for you. There's a needle waitin' and yards o' sail to be fixed. Come wi' me.'

'Wraaf. Wraaff. Wraafff!' A torrent of barking came from the rocks.

'Oh no, that's Gregor!' exclaimed Isabel. 'I have to go. Suzie's in trouble.' She jumped to her feet as Cutlass dragged Tom towards the beach huts.

'Gregor trod on a craaab!' shrieked Suzie from beyond the rocks.

'I won't be a minute!' Isabel called to her. She blinked. Cutlass and the boy had already gone. Damp footprints led away, fading quickly in the heat.

'Quiiick!' yelled Suzie.

She found her sister sitting by a deep blue rock pool, with a limp Gregor lying beside her wearing Suzie's hat and an eye patch.

'He's a pirate dog now. We nearly caught a crab with great big pincers.'

Gregor held up his paw and whined. Isabel examined it and ruffled his fur. 'You look fine. I expect it just nipped you.'

'Owh,' whimpered Gregor.

Isabel took off his hat and eye patch, clipped on his lead and tugged gently. Gregor sat with his head lowered, looking sadly at the ground.

Suzie shook her head. 'I tried that. He won't come wiv me. He's too upset. He's Blackbeard the pirate dog and that crab hurt his feelings.'

'I guess I'll have to carry him.'

Suzie tipped a bucket full of crabs into the rock pool and Isabel picked up Gregor, who sneezed loudly in her ear.

'Come on, Suzie, we'll take him home.'

But Suzie was already heading in the opposite direction. 'I won't be long. I want to see the puffins. You'll take ages carrying Gregor anyway,' she insisted.

'Oh, OK,' gulped Isabel. 'You can tell Ben what happened to Gregor. But don't go near the sea, there's a mermaid.'

'*Is* there? *Really*?' Suzie's eyes lit up. She licked her lips and looked around hopefully.

CHAPTER THREE

CLIMBING THE
CAT O' NINE TAILS

Isabel and Suzie arrived home with a very tired Gregor to find a huge white van parked in the driveway of their cottage. *Jolly Roger* was painted in large black letters on the side with a skull and crossbones, and a crooked chimney pipe poked from the roof.

'Alfie and Peggy are here!' called Isabel's mother from the kitchen, where she was reading a heap of cookery books with her glasses sliding down her nose. The door in the side of the van stood open. Suzie and Isabel peered inside at a small wood-burning stove and a bed set on a ledge. The floor was covered with piles of red and blue climbing rope, harnesses and silver clips.

Their mother's old school friend, Peggy, greeted them at the kitchen door, hugging the two girls. Suzie stared at her stripy headscarf and purple shorts. 'What a lovely dog!' cried Peggy. 'He can come in the *Jolly Roger* with us!' Gregor ignored her and sank in a heap under the table. Alfie was surrounded by piles of rope and various climbers' clips and bolts. He was tanned and thin, with strong arms that tapered to hands with long slender fingers, like a music teacher's. He smiled at Isabel, humming as he coiled the ropes.

'Izzie loves climbing with us,' Peggy said to Isabel's mother. 'Of course, we have to keep away from the areas where the puffins and peregrine falcons nest. We'll do the *Cat o' Nine Tails* climb with you, Izzie, near Blacknor. The weather's perfect. I brought my camera to take pictures.'

Peggy twiddled the camera around her neck. 'Here's a shot I took of the sky above Portland earlier today.' She tucked her braided fair hair into her scarf. Isabel peered over her shoulder. 'Look, in the clouds over Lyme Bay, a ship with tattered sails, masts and ropes. Alfie says it looks like a pirate ship.'

'I wanna see!' bellowed Suzie. 'I'm the pirate round here.' Peggy showed Suzie the picture while Isabel looked at Alfie with a frown. He was busying himself with climbing ropes.

Mrs Maydew sank on to a chair beside Peggy, wearing her favourite anchor earrings. 'I'd come climbing with you, but I'm far too busy. I have to start the birthday cake. It always takes ages. And you're too young,' she added to Suzie, who was still fingering a rope.

Suzie scowled at her. 'I'm 5 now!' she shouted, 'an' I run *Maydew's Moggies*.' A fluffy tom-cat peeped over the edge of his box and miaowed.

Her mother rubbed her forehead. 'Yes, and it costs a fortune to feed all the cats. Our food bills have gone through the roof,' she said, turning to rummage in the cupboards for an enormous mixing bowl. She appeared with wooden spoons, a cake bowl and two bags of flour.

'It's getting late. I'd better take Gregor back to Groves Farm,' Isabel said. She wanted to take a look around. Portland pirates, who belonged in 1691, were wandering the Isle. The *Fortune* lurked somewhere along the coast too. Isabel had a horrible feeling that the mermaid was right; somehow *she* had brought the pirates into the present day.

CHAPTER FOUR

A SMUGGLER RETURNS

Mrs Greychurch opened the garden gate of a cottage on Weston Street, tucked on the far edge of land that had once belonged to Groves Farm, beyond the two mediaeval windmills. The roof of the cottage sloped down low and fat chickens ran around the yard. She ducked under the shady branches of the apple and pear trees that lined the garden path. A large green budgie whistled at her from a high branch.

'Shooo!' Mrs Greychurch waved her handbag at the annoying bird. At the door of the cottage she was greeted by Penfold Lucke, a tall, slender young man with soggy dishwater eyes, who she visited on Wednesdays for tea.

'That budgie's been around for days,' Penfold explained. 'I've fed him seeds and hung a cuttlefish in the tree. Come in. I'm glad you don't have Gregor today. Your daughter Miranda brought him along and he ate all my biscuits.'

'Gregor *is* fond of biscuits, I'm afraid,' said Mrs Greychurch, elbowing by him through the door and barrelling into the comfortable lounge papered with red roses. She sank into the flouncy sofa, fanning her pink cheeks. 'It's terribly warm today.'

Penfold sat in the chair opposite and crossed his legs. Mrs Greychurch's eyebrows shot up. He wore thin strappy sandals and his toenails were painted gold.

'Are you enjoying the summer?' she asked politely. Penfold flicked his floppy fringe from his eyes.

'Oh yes. I'm on holiday from the library for 2 weeks.'

'Your mother and I are great friends. Such a shame she moved to Spain. I promised I'd keep an eye on you,' said Mrs Greychurch, eyeing his toenails.

'I want to talk to you about the pirates,' said Penfold, leaning forward. 'Only yesterday I saw a pirate ship off the Bill with three great masts and a carved mermaid figurehead, just like the ship described in the *Echo*.'

At the mention of the mermaid, Mrs Greychurch snorted. 'Pfff, pirates,' she exclaimed. 'Villains and vagabonds. I've got just the thing for them – a cannon! See how their ship fares against a real gun.'

Penfold clutched her hand. 'Mrs Greychurch, I want to find this ship. It's very important to me. I've always felt that I'm destined to meet these pirates and write their story. It could be a best seller. *Portland Pirates*! I am a writer you know.' He pointed to the row of *Pirate Friend* magazines on the shelf. 'My short stories are very popular.'

'I run a pirate look-out,' sniffed Mrs Greychurch, tugging her hand free from Penfold's clutch. Thunder rolled above them, shaking the windows. She glanced up at the roof. 'I don't like the sound of that.' She patted her forehead with a handkerchief, feeling hotter and hotter.

'Neither do I. I'd better get the chickens into the hen house,' said Penfold.

Mrs Greychurch struggled to her feet and straightened her orange skirt, patterned with sovereigns and fish. She rifled in her handbag. 'Here's my new *Pirate Watch* newsletter. If you spot any pirate ships again, let me know. My number's at the foot of the page.'

It was swelteringly hot at tea time when Isabel and Gregor arrived at Groves Farm. They walked under the Groves oak tree, the leaves burnt gold by the relentless sun. Gregor flopped in the shade and rested. Isabel looked across at the farmhouse. The farm was at the heart of Portland, lying between the town of Easton and the old windmills, where farmlands had sprawled for hundreds of years. Her mother's cousin, Mrs Groves, ran Groves riding stables, as well as tending older horses who had retired to the farm fields. The farmhouse itself was a long rambling building with teetering chimneys, full of paintings and chunky old furniture. Mrs Groves never threw anything away.

Isabel walked slowly towards the house, still thinking about the cabin boy and the strange pirate, Cutlass. Gregor bounded ahead through the kitchen door and into the lounge, to find Mrs Groves draped on the sofa suffering from summer flu. The curtains were still drawn. Wearing a dressing gown and scuffed blue slippers, her wavy fair hair unbrushed, Mrs Groves opened one eye. 'Is that you, Gregor?' Gregor hurtled across the room and leaped on Mrs Groves. He growled and wrestled with the edge of her gown. Isabel glanced at a pile of bills lying in the middle of the coffee table, gathering dust.

'Thank you for bringing him home, Isabel. I'll put out his tea,' said Mrs Groves. She tottered into the kitchen, leaving Isabel to wrestle a cushion from Gregor. Mrs Groves tipped dog biscuits into a bowl and put out fresh water for Gregor, then sank into a kitchen chair. Sunlight glinted through the smeary window, the kitchen as stuffy as the cabin of a ship. Feeling feverish, she rested her head on her hand and dozed.

Isabel peered through the doorway and Gregor sat down next to Mrs Groves. He scratched his ear, then nibbled the edge of her dressing gown and whined. As Mrs Groves seemed to be asleep, Isabel wandered into the dining room, where rows of books about rearing sheep and tending horses lined the room. 'The Well Beloved by Thomas Hardy,' she read aloud, opening the book near the beginning at 'Home of the Slingers.' She remembered that the first inhabitants of Portland were famed for slinging rocks at invaders. She read a little, then put the book back on the shelf and toyed with *Moonfleet* by JM Falkner, admiring the cover picture of a ship caught in huge waves off Chesil Beach.

She felt the eyes of the Groves' ancestors staring from a row of paintings. A tall man in a billowing coat stood by the Groves oak tree. 'Flintlock Groves 1691,' she read from a small bronze plaque. In the shade of the tree, she saw tumbled barrels and caskets. In his hand, Flintlock held a trickle of silver chain. 'I expect he smuggled goods in and out of Groves Farm,' decided Isabel, remembering that Mrs Groves' always claimed to have smugglers in her family history.

She took *Moonfleet* and sat at the kitchen table. Gregor put his nose in her lap, gazing up at her as she read. She would stay until 9 o'clock when Mrs Greychurch, Mrs Groves' friend, usually called in. Every now and then, Isabel glanced at the sleeping Mrs Groves. Thunder rumbled around the island, like cannons firing from a distant ship. The sky in the window shifted colour from rose grey to purple, and slowly the night arrived to hide the sky with fragile summer darkness.

Flintlock kicked the black horse on, urging him into a gallop. He shot though the dusk, a shadow against the deep violet sky. His horse's hooves thundered as he rode through the trees, weaving and cutting across, changing direction as he took the steep hill behind St Andrew's Church. At the top of the slope he reined in. The silver coins, candlesticks, flasks of brandy and bundles of lace were tucked into saddle bags draped across his horse. Despite the sea storm, a fishing boat had brought him back from France where he had traded valuable wool from his Portland sheep for silver and lace.

The horse's breath steamed in the night air. He had lost the Revenue men in the woods beyond Church Ope Cove, a grim troop of men who worked for the Board of Customs, a smuggler's enemies. Looking back across the curving bay of Church Ope, he saw a ship sailing towards the cove, its sails ragged from the recent storm. 'Well, well,' he mused, 'so the *Fortune*'s back at last.'

Flintlock turned his horse towards the heart of the Isle, taking the darkest winding paths, heading home to his farm. 'I'll find Red Pete tomorrow,' he determined. He rode into the stable yard beside the farmhouse as the stars lit up the sky. He yawned and stretched his arms, loosening the dark blue cloak at his throat. He was on home ground now and glad to be back. Yet the stables seemed quiet and his busy working farm unusually silent, even for the late hour. Surely the maids would still be at work, clearing dishes and setting firewood in the hearths for the morning.

'Where are ye?' he roared.

He strode into the farmhouse kitchen, slamming the door behind him. Mrs Groves yelped and fell off the kitchen chair. Gregor shot behind her, trying to hide under her dressing gown. The intruder stared at them.

'What are ye doing in my house?' he demanded.

Mrs Groves struggled to her feet, her face fiery pink. 'How dare you come in here? This is private property! See him off Gregor!' The dog peered at the intruder from behind her knees with wide, scared eyes.

Flintlock stamped past her to the lounge, with Mrs Groves following close behind. She grabbed a sturdy wooden pole from a dusty corner by the fireplace and brandished it at Flintlock.

'Get out!' she yelled.

He snatched the pole from her and stared at it. 'My own Portland Reeve staff from the Court Leet, who govern the Isle. Here are the very marks i' the wood I made meself.' He gazed around the room. 'This is *my* farm. Is this some wicked enchantment? Are ye a witch?'

'Good heavens!' said Mrs Groves. 'No one has *ever* spoken to me like that in my own home!'

She snatched a copper pan from the fireplace and swung it, clanging Flintlock on the side of the head with a loud *pdoyng*. He sat down abruptly in a shabby armchair, his eyes still roving round the room. He rubbed his head. For several seconds, Flintlock and

Mrs Groves looked at one another. He took in her old gown and slippers. Mrs Groves noted his dark Groves' eyes, fine cloak and trimmed beard.

'Odd,' said the smuggler, after a while. 'Ye have a look o' my mother, God rest her soul. Ye *must* be an aunt. That's the only explanation. For this is *my* farm. I left it but three weeks gone to fetch goods from France.' He touched his head again where she had hit him.

'I can assure you, young man, this farmhouse is *mine*,' said Mrs Groves indignantly.

Flintlock noticed the bills on the table, grabbed the pile of papers and rummaged through them. 'How much?' he exclaimed. 'For shoeing horses! I never heard such a fee. And this figure to repair a stone wall? I can do this work meself.'

Mrs Groves began to feel a bit better about the intruder. She told herself the man must be a distant cousin paying a visit. She sank on to the sofa and Gregor huddled by her feet.

'Well, Aunt ...?'

'... Estelle,' said Mrs Groves, trying to smooth her tangled hair.

'Aunt Estelle, I little thought to return home and find Groves Farm so godforsaken. We will have to do what we can to fix the place.'

An hour later, Flintlock was still pacing the farmhouse. He tugged the curtains back and peered out into the dark yard. He looked into every room and cupboard and ran up the stairs, taking them two at a time. Mrs Groves could hear his heavy boots clumping as he stormed across the bedrooms, slamming doors. Then the sound of taps switching on and off in the bathroom, as if he had never seen running water before. Mrs Groves wiped her nose.

'Who sleeps in *my* room?' demanded Flintlock from the doorway, glaring at her.

'I think you'll find it is my bedroom. I have several guest rooms,' dithered Mrs Groves.

'Well, have a bed made up, good woman.' He made for the door again, calling back to her, 'Take the silver candlesticks. Sell 'em at the market. Mention no names, though. And I'd like a decent meal o' the morrow, no mutton mind. Good beef and all the trimmings. I will bathe in that strange apparatus ye have up yonder.' He ran upstairs again.

'Well,' said Mrs Groves, looking at the elegant candlesticks. She heard water run and singing from the bathroom. She blinked. Somehow, she was starting to feel much better after her flu.

'Gregor? I'll put you to bed in a minute, after I've given you a brush. Your fur is scruffy,' she said bossily, as she swept past him to fetch the brush. 'We've quite a few things to do tomorrow. I should be able to sell those candlesticks in Dorchester. It'll pay for the horses' bills, at least.'

Gregor panted happily. He enjoyed travelling along Chesil Beach first thing in the morning, hanging his head out of the Land Rover window and racing the kitesurfers along Portland Harbour.

CHAPTER FIVE

RED PETE LOSES HIS SHIP

'Where 'ave them seadogs gone?' roared Pirate Captain Red Pete. He dropped the sacks of treasure and ran through the dark woods above Church Ope Cove, looking at the sweep of sea below him. His ship, the *Fortune*, anchored just a few hours earlier near Cheyne Weares, had suddenly vanished. He unsheathed his sword, pulled the long black coat around him and tugged his tricorn hat low over his eyes. Waves hushed against the grey pebbles. 'I shouldn't have left me ship to seek out the boy. Not with the Siren lurkin' off these shores.'

The woods were strange and unfamiliar in the pale moonlight. Ivy curled around his ankles as he tapped an old chestnut tree with his sword. 'I know this ole tree where a lazy owl sleeps.' Eyes blinked dozily at him from a hole in the trunk. Red Pete shook his head, angry and puzzled. After attacking a ship bound for Plymouth, he had sailed the *Fortune* across Lyme Bay. Suddenly the dark shape of Portland had appeared ahead and powerful tides had pulled the ship towards the Isle. He had heard the Siren singing as they sailed closer and closer. He always dreaded the place, knowing that the sea witch would be watching and waiting for him.

Then a bank of storm clouds chased the ship from the south-west. He had ridden the worst of the gale before the storm caught them by the southerly tip of Portland, the Beal. They had nearly sunk beneath crashing waves before reaching the sheltered east of the Isle, their sails in tatters. Anchored a few cables off Cheyne Weares, he realised the cabin boy was missing. 'Told 'im to stay below in the hold. No sea legs on 'im.' The pirate scratched his fiery red beard and stared at Rufus Castle, a sturdy old castle keep overlooking the deserted beach. 'Tom'll turn up. The Siren will make sure o' that,' he said to himself.

He grasped the sacks of treasure that he had rowed ashore and headed for a low cave hidden by rocks just to the south of Church Ope. Ducking beneath a hanging rock, he found a dry space on the sandy floor. He put the heavy sacks against the far wall. The ship had been overladen with valuable cargo, slowing their passage.

'Silk, spices, finest tea, an' a weight o' gold an' silver coins. O' course, I left the barrels o' wine an' brandy aboard, as well as me new sails.' The barrels were from a foolish Spanish merchant ship. Red Pete had pirated their cargo with little fuss. Everyone knew him as a fair pirate, plying his trade from Spanish Cadiz, up the French coast and north along to the English Channel.

Leaving the cave, he noticed that the tarred boathouse at Church Ope had gone, and the fishing boats. Even the slipway for sending Portland stone to London had disappeared. He headed into the woods, kicking his feet through long tendrils of ivy. The darkness was different. There was an orange glow in the sky and coloured lights moved over him. 'Like lost souls seekin' heaven,' he murmured. He even thought he heard one roar in the distance. 'Could do wi' a sniff of brandy,' he mumbled. He wandered through the trees, listening to the owl hooting.

The Mermaid Inn was in deep darkness. Red Pete pressed his nose to the window. 'T'ain't that late,' he sighed. He would have to find someone with a bottle in the cupboard. 'An angel to aid a weary wanderer who's lost 'is ship,' he thought.

He walked along the narrow road. Turning the corner he stopped abruptly.

'What in heaven's name is that?' A lamp glowed at the top of a pole. Red Pete edged around the streetlight, holding his sword. Surely a barmaid lived hereabouts. He banged on the nearest door.

'Open up!' he yelled. A light flicked on and the door opened. Red Pete pushed past. 'About time, woman. 'Tis Red Pete ye be keepin' waiting. Bring out the brandy, I've 'ad a terrible night o' it. Tom

Lucke's nothin' but trouble and the evil Siren's lured me ship 'n' crew away.' He threw himself into a comfortable chair. Mrs Greychurch stood at the doorway in a huge green night-dress, her mouth open in an 'O'.

She was a fine woman, Red Pete thought, built like a ship in full sail. He took in the room, nice and cosy. He had fallen on his feet here. A bottle stood on a side table. The pirate leaned over and helped himself to a swig.

Mrs Greychurch clutched her nightgown to her chin. 'Who are you?'

'A poor ole captain what's lost 'is ship. Now come an' sit down an' I'll sing a song that'll make yer hair curl.'

Within minutes, Red Pete was snoring loudly in the chair. Mrs Greychurch perched opposite him, staring. 'A captain. Perhaps pirates took his ship,' she said thoughtfully. But she didn't like the look of him, with his long coat and bushy red beard. She poked him. Red Pete didn't stir. 'I'll have to deal with him in the morning,' she huffed.

CHAPTER SIX
MIRANDA MEETS A SMUGGLER

The following morning, Miranda Greychurch sauntered along the lane near Groves Farm. She paused at the top of a hill. Ahead of her was the Groves Farm tree, a towering oak with crinkled leaves rippling in the soft breeze. Sunlight sparkled around the tree. A tiny warbler sang in the highest branches. 'I can't think with all that awful birdsong!' she sniffed, wiping her nose on the sleeve of her shirt.

Miranda pulled sunglasses out of her bag and plonked them on her nose. She picked her way along the overgrown path, winding through the field towards Groves Farm. Bees hummed and the powerful scent of yellow flowers wafted in the air. Miranda sneezed and stopped to blow her nose. Skylarks twittered overhead. She glared at the sky. 'Shut uuup! Oh, how I hate summer!'

'Now, now, that's a poor use for the King's English.' A man with a beard was walking towards her, wearing a tall black hat set with a buckle. Miranda stared. Surely that was a sword tied to a belt around his waist, over dark breeches. A huge black horse followed him. 'I'll walk awhile wi' ye to Groves Farmhouse. Have ye seen the *Fortune*? I cannot find the vessel nor Red Pete, its cap'n. Yet I clearly saw his ship last night. I'm Flintlock Groves of Groves Farm. Ye must be one o' the peasant girls from the farm cottages.'

Shocked, Miranda tripped over a bramble. 'Flintlock *Groves*?' she repeated.

Indeed, *I* will lead the way, as you've proved so hopeless. My good mother always sent her maids to yon island day school, or they end with no more sense 'n a cuckoo.' He bounded on to the

24

horse. 'Follow me.'

He led Miranda along the narrow footpath and soon the lopsided chimneys of the farmhouse were in sight. Miranda puffed along behind the horse.

At the stables, Gregor was waiting, his tail waving like a flag. He hurled himself at Miranda, barking furiously, delighted to see her. Mrs Groves was waiting too. She smoothed her hair with the palm of her hand. Miranda stared at her. She had never seen Mrs Groves in a dress before, especially one patterned with pink starfish. In fact, thought Miranda, she had barely seen Mrs Groves move for days.

'Lunch is ready,' she announced. Miranda's face was beetroot red. 'I'll get you some cold water, Miranda.'

Flintlock strode ahead of them into the farmhouse. 'Take a seat, Aunt Estelle, and rest yerself. The girl can serve dinner. She seems to have been lost in the fields. Little wonder, she looks underfed. And what ridiculous garb to walk out in. Your housemaid, I presume?'

Mrs Groves and Miranda exchanged looks. Flintlock seated himself at the dining table, where dishes of vegetables and roast beef steamed. Paintings of the Groves family through history gazed down from the walls.

'Come along,' he said. 'The food grows cold. I'll have a slice o' this fine beef, good woman. Ye may see to my horse shortly. Maid, fetch the sauces from the kitchen.'

As Flintlock ate, Mrs Groves nibbled a carrot and stared over his head at a portrait dated 1691 of a daring smuggler by the Groves oak tree. She gulped.

'A fine painting o' me,' he said, still chewing. 'Have ye heard any news o' Cap'n Red Pete?' Mrs Groves shook her head.

'I saw th' *Fortune* clear as anythin' last night off the Weares. Red Pete runs a skull and crossbones up the mast. The Revenue men can't take 'im. Too many cannon. He pirates just as he likes, from Normandy to the Bay o' Biscay an' along the coast o' Dorset. Never lingers by th' Isle – they say 'e fears the song o' the Siren.' Flintlock looked thoughtful. 'I must find Red Pete, soon as I can.'

'We're not keen on pirates here on Portland,' commented Mrs Groves.

'P'raps not, yet the Isle of Portland was named for the Saxon pirate, Portus, who landed at Church Ope long ago.'

Miranda returned and plonked a jug of gravy in front of Flintlock.

'Take care!' he bellowed. 'My mother sends her maids to the new school named for Saint George along Rayfourn, where a Miss Maydew takes the classes.'

'D'you mean the St George's Centre?' puzzled Mrs Groves.

'Aye. You've been lax to let 'er schooling slide. She's no more sense 'n a clothes-peg.'

Flintlock talked non-stop as he ate, waving his fork at them. He had a number of jobs in mind. First, the run-down fences and walls of the farm would be repaired. The horses in the stables were overfed and should be ridden more. That letter on the table from the Revenue, they would have to pay that sum forthwith, he didn't want them prying. Gregor sneaked into the dining room and wrapped himself around Flintlock's leg, resting his head on his knee. Every now and then, Flintlock passed him a piece of meat beneath the table.

'An' your sheepdog's in shocking shape. What do you feed the poor beast? Look at his girth! Put him to work. A lazy dog is no use to any farm. Read me the date from the calendar again.'

Mrs Groves gulped. 'July 25th.'

'1691, o' course.'

Mrs Groves cleared her throat, 'A little later than that.'

'Never!' shouted Flintlock, dropping his knife with a clatter. He looked from Miranda to Mrs Groves in horror. 'Our Regents William and Mary are still with us, surely? The Protestants must hold firm for England.'

'Our Queen is Elizabeth,' interrupted Miranda.

'Good Queen Bess. Defeated the Spanish Armada. Fond o' pirates, so they say.' He leaned across the table to Mrs Groves. 'Died in 1603, ages ago. Clearly this poor girl needs to go to school.' He turned to Miranda. 'In Queen Jane's closet at Portland Castle, ye may read, *God save Kinge Henri the 8 of that name ... and the Ladi Elizabet*. We're a Royal Manor here, always will be.'

Flintlock flung down the tea towel that he had used as a napkin. Mrs Groves and Miranda watched him stride from the room.

'I'll help you wash up, Mrs Groves,' said Miranda, piling up the plates.

'Yes,' said Mrs Groves, vaguely. She stared at the painting of Flintlock Groves. Had he really travelled to Groves Farm from over 300 years ago? She shook her head. 'Better not mention Flintlock to your mother,' she said to Miranda. Mrs Greychurch would not approve of a smuggler from the 17th century.

As she bustled to the kitchen, thunder shook the building and the kitchen window rattled. Mrs Groves peered out at the yard, wondering if a cooling rainstorm would follow. She drummed her fingers on the draining board. If Flintlock had really travelled so far across time, who else might follow him from the past?

CHAPTER SEVEN

A MAYDEW WITCH

Ryder, a local windsurfer, was standing with his climber friend Alfie in the driveway outside Isabel's house, scratching his head. His fluffy hair stood on end and he wore a baggy t-shirt and enormous blue shorts. His eyes were screwed up, his nostrils flaring with excitement.

'Yeah, I know the climbs around Portland very well, Alfredo. We could start with *Yikes Shaggy*.' He jabbed the map on the bonnet of his van, folded to show the west coast of Portland. His VW camper, loaded with surfboards, was parked behind Alfie's *Jolly Roger* van. *Windcool* was painted on the side over a curling blue wave. Ryder had trained Wolven Groves for the Olympics and was now running a windsurfing school at Osprey Quay.

Alfie rubbed his nose thoughtfully. '*Reptile Smile*'s a great climb too.'

Suzie trotted around the flowerbeds in her pirate outfit, glaring at Ryder. 'Why's he allowed to go climbing wiv Uncle Alfie and Aunt Peggy and I can't?' she muttered, angrily soaking the rose bushes with water from her watering can.

Ben leaned against the garden wall, staring at his iPhone. He tapped the screen with a finger, frowning. Isabel watched over his shoulder. Nellie, the black cat, twined herself around her ankles.

Ben glanced up. 'Suzie still doesn't like Ryder, the Surf Dinosaur,' he commented.

'Why d'you say that?' asked Isabel

'She's emptied the watering can over his feet.'

Ryder, unconcerned, was still talking to Alfie, shaking drops of water from his flip-flops.

'Suzie!' called Isabel. Her sister dropped the watering can and waved a sponge at her. She dipped the sponge in a bucket of soapy water and scrubbed Alfie's van busily. By the kitchen window, her mother was measuring flour, sugar and butter into some enormous scales. There were trays of eggs stacked around her.

'I have to cycle to the Bill today,' said Isabel to Ben.

'Wha' for?' asked Ben, still staring at his iPhone. 'This is a great app. I can look at the volcanoes in Iceland.'

'I'm looking for pirates and a ship called the *Fortune*.'

Ben glanced up. 'This is another of your weird things, isn't it? I can't believe you're still looking for fairies, mermaids and pirate ships.'

'I've found fairies, mermaids *and* dragons!'

Ben argued. 'You've seen a hawk moth, a dolphin, and a ....'

'Exactly – you can't explain the dragon. Even Mrs Greychurch saw him.'

Ben gave Isabel a look. 'Mrs Greychurch sees a lot of things.'

Peggy rushed into the garden and hugged Isabel. 'Fantastic news, Izzie. I hear we're all going climbing soon. Ryder's coming too.'

'I wanna come,' yelled Suzie, flinging down her sponge.

'Of course, dear, when you're bigger,' said Peggy kindly.

'I wonder if a chocolate cake would be better. I'll have to buy some cooking chocolate,' called Isabel's mother from the kitchen window, rubbing flour over her forehead. She started counting the eggs again.

Ryder pointed to the map, continuing his conversation with Alfie. 'How about if we go through the Cuttings by the old Mermaid Inn and climb round there, Alfredo?'

'Good weather for it,' said Alfie thoughtfully.

'I have to go out today,' Isabel butted in quickly.

'I wanna go too! There's a pirate ship out there and I wanna find it with Isabel!' shrieked Suzie, clinging to Isabel's leg.

Peggy gently untwined Suzie. 'You can be a cabin person today with me. We can shiver me timbers and mop the decks.' As Isabel collected a bottle of water, Suzie was swirling water around the kitchen floor with a mop, making swooshing sounds.

'See y' later,' said Ben. 'Let me know if you find your pirates. I've never seen a pirate ship anywhere near Portland. Of course, neither has anyone else. Real pirates haven't sailed these seas for hundreds of years.'

'There *are* pirates!' Suzie insisted, washing her mop over Ben's feet, 'and I'm gonna join 'em soon.'

Isabel followed the cliff path along the west coast, the handlebars of her mountain bike jolting at every bump and tussock of grass. To one side, the fields stretched away peacefully, Portland sheep grazing in the distance. On the other, cliffs tumbled in a sheer hazardous drop to the sea, the aquamarine water edged with white froth. Isabel steered around a corner and bounced over a small hill. Ahead loomed the lighthouse, vivid red and white against the blue sky. She shot down the slope, going left towards the Old Lower Lighthouse, and bumped along the stony path to the rows of colourful beach huts overlooking the sea.

'Stop!' shrieked Mrs Greychurch, in a flowery summer dress and large red wellies. 'This is a no cycling zone.'

'I don't think so,' said Isabel, narrowly missing her. Respectfully she climbed off her bicycle and placed it carefully between herself and Mrs Greychurch.

'People should be able to enjoy the summer without worrying about careless cyclists.' Mrs Greychurch looked down at her, her lips quivering. 'All around you, there's piracy, affray and grand theft auto. Isn't it time you helped put a stop to it? Think about it, Isabel.' She fixed Isabel with a beady stare.

'I *am* thinking about it, Mrs Greychurch,' said Isabel politely.

Satisfied, Mrs Greychurch disappeared into her hut, like a spider retreating to its web. She slammed the door and pulled the curtains against the sunlight.

Isabel took a swig from her water bottle. Along the horizon, the sea and sky met in a line of shimmering blue, melting together. Isabel left her bike at the edge of the beach huts and walked to the sea. To the south, the Portland *Race* churned with white froth, a deadly clash of currents, and in the distance she saw the white Condor ferry scurrying to Guernsey like a small ghost. Beneath the gleaming sea lay broken shipwrecks. Isabel shuddered. The *Fortune* had sailed these treacherous waters with Red Pete at the helm. Further along the shore, Isabel saw a man in a tall hat with a black horse. Like her, he was gazing out to sea, searching the horizon.

A voice made her jump. 'You disappeared,' called Tom. The cabin boy stood behind her on the windswept grass, a westerly breeze tugging at his shirt.

'What happened to Cutlass?'

He shifted uneasily from one foot to the other. 'Our ship's carpenter? He's gone a'lookin' for the *Fortune*. The ship's vanished. I slipped away from him, walked round th' Grove an' along the shore to St Andrew's, but our church has gone too. Just ruins, as though a giant came i' the night an' shook it all to pieces. I hardly know the village o' Weston.'

'It's a different time. You must have travelled across time during the storm,' suggested Isabel gently. She struggled to find words to describe what had happened to Tom. She remembered her own journeys to the 17th-century Isle of Portland, where the windmills in the fields at Top Growlands turned in the breeze and smugglers rode across a moonlit isle.

The boy rubbed his eyes. 'T'was a weird, magical storm. Waves as high as St Andrew's bell tower lashed our ship before even the wind changed. I remember a stowaway by the bow.' He turned to her, his eyes narrow. 'Tell me, who exactly *are* you?'

'I'm Isabel Maydew.'

'Maydew!' exclaimed the boy, stumbling away from her, 'like the island witch, who called fearsome dragons from the sea.' Thunder rumbled across the sky, shaking the ground. Heavy drops of warm summer rain left smudges across Tom's face and arms. He backed further away from her, his face white with fear. 'You cast a spell, lurin' the *Fortune* into that terrible storm. Seekin' her treasure, were ye? You're a fiend and a witch!' Tom turned and ran from her, disappearing between the beach huts.

'Wait a minute!' called Isabel.

'Where did he go?' The man leading the black horse had reached Isabel just as Tom disappeared. He grabbed her arm. 'What's become of Red Pete and the *Fortune*? I know that lad! He's one o' Red Pete's scragtail pirates!' Isabel stared at his tall hat set with a silver buckle and his dark blue woollen cape. 'Come on, girl, lost your tongue?' The man shook her angrily. 'If you see him again, tell 'im Flintlock Groves wants a word in 'is ear.' He put his boot in the silver stirrup, gripped the reins and sprung on to his powerful horse.

'Flintlock Groves!' gasped Isabel, as he rode away. 'Mrs Groves' ancestor, from the painting at Groves Farm. A cabin boy, pirates, and now there's a smuggler too!'

CHAPTER EIGHT
PIRATE WATCH

Mrs Greychurch dusted around the plant pots on a windowsill that overlooked the narrow road to Church Ope Cove. The sycamore trees glistened and a fall of summer rain had left the skies swept clean and sparkling blue. Blackbirds sang in a garden full of golden marigolds and pink roses. She pondered how best she should spend her day. The captain had wolfed down breakfast before she could accuse him of being a pirate, and left with a promise to 'Bring 'er a piece o' nice lace'. Miranda had also left in a rush, wearing her riding gear, to help out at the stables at Groves Farm.

Mrs Greychurch slipped on her sensible walking shoes, shut the shiny red door behind her and walked towards Rufus Castle. There she took the coast path, staying alert for signs of pirates. They could be anywhere; breaking into beach huts, or creeping into the supermarket to steal bread rolls. It was hard to know where to begin her search. She walked briskly along the overgrown footpaths of the Cuttings to follow the long path that meandered between the cliffs and the sea. Orange buds bloomed on the gorse bushes and tiny pink and blue flowers peeked from the rocks, alongside red poppies wilting in the heat.

On the rocky cliffs she spotted two climbers. A woman with messy hair stood nearby, taking photographs. Beside her, Mrs Greychurch saw a small pirate, Suzie Maydew. 'Excuse me!' she called, bustling towards them. 'D'you have permission to climb here?'

'Of course,' said Peggy, gripping Mrs Greychurch by the hand and shaking it firmly. Mrs Greychurch looked distastefully at her purple shorts. Ryder and Alfie were scaling the cliffs above them, watched by several goats that lived on the Weares. Mrs Greychurch shielded her eyes to view the climbers. Alfie climbed like a mountain cat, leading Ryder.

'I've set up a *Pirate Watch* to keep an eye on the island,' announced Mrs Greychurch.

'Ah, I read in the newspaper there was some trouble with pirates,' said Peggy. She took another photo of Ryder.

'He's nearly at the top,' called Suzie excitedly. 'Can we leave him up there and go home?'

'I don't trust those animals,' resumed Mrs Greychurch, glaring at the goats. 'They always look at me strangely.'

'Maaaa,' agreed a long-haired goat with curling horns.

'You can never tell what they're thinking, unlike our dear gentle Portland sheep,' Mrs Greychurch continued. She watched Ryder clamber to the top of the cliff. He waved to them. Mrs Greychurch tutted disapprovingly.

'I like Portland sheep too,' said Suzie, tugging at her skirt.

'Yes, I hear you kept a sheep in your garden. Sheep stealing's a crime, young lady,' snapped Mrs Greychurch.

Peggy put down her camera and set off to collect the ropes and clips left at the foot of the cliff. 'Ryder's taking the footpath down from the top,' she called. Mrs Greychurch put her hands on her hips and watched Ryder skidding down the narrow cliff path. A cat stuck a sleepy head out of the basket beside Suzie and miaowed.

'Has that cat had its jabs?' she demanded.

''Course,' said Suzie, hauling the large tabby cat out of the basket and hugging him. 'Groover hates being left at home, he gets lonely,' she explained. 'I'm trying to find a nice home for him.'

'Well, I don't want a cat. I'm too busy looking out for pirates,' noted Mrs Greychurch. 'No doubt there's treasure hidden all over Portland by now, like fleas on some old moggie.' Suzie's eyes grew round. Her mouth fell open. She pointed over Mrs Greychurch's shoulder. 'Gold coins and fine jewels tucked in every nook and cranny,' continued Mrs Greychurch. She heard a scuffle of feet behind her and turned slowly to face a pirate with a blue scarf knotted around his head. She gulped and raised her hands.

The pirate pointed a sword at Mrs Greychurch, his strange watery eyes fixed on her. 'Where is it?' he snarled. 'Where's Red Pete hidden me treasure?'

Mrs Greychurch gaped at the pirate, her mouth opening and closing like a large fish.

Suzie unsheathed a plastic sword from her belt. 'Take that!' she cried, waving her weapon at the pirate. She flipped the pirate's sword aside and jumped around him. Ryder appeared from the footpath and walked over to them in his climbing hat and harness. He sat on a rock.

'You must be a pirate, dude,' he said.

'Ooh, a pirate,' said Peggy, 'how exciting. Can I take your photo?' Cutlass slipped away as Peggy tried to snap a shot of him. 'That's very odd,' she said, peering at the screen. 'How did I miss him? He's not in the picture.'

Mrs Greychurch was snorting with fury, her chins wobbling. 'Attacked in broad daylight!' she quivered at last. 'Outrageous! That's it! I'm setting up my cannon right now.'

Alfie had finished winding the climbing ropes around his arm in large loops and now sprang from rock to rock to reach them. 'Did *you* see the pirate?' asked Peggy.

Alfie nodded.

Mrs Greychurch looked him up and down. 'Was that awful man a friend of yours? Well, I shall report him as soon as I get home. And I can't see the point of rock climbing either,' she sniffed. 'I've suggested to the Council that a nice cable car up and down these cliffs would be very popular. Like the one in Bournemouth. It attracts a better class of visitor.' She looked at Ryder, whose ripped t-shirt sported a blue windsurfing sail and faded letters. '*Windcool* indeed,' she snorted.

Isabel had ridden from Groves Farm stables on Isaac, her favourite chestnut horse. She followed the grassy paths south along the Weares, looking out for the pirate ship, the *Fortune*. The rain had cleared, leaving the sky vivid blue with seagulls wheeling high above her. In the distance, she glimpsed the Needles at the western end of the Isle of Wight. She turned away from the sea and trotted Isaac through an abandoned quarry onto a path overgrown with spiky brambles and red blackberries. Long tendrils of bindweed curled across the way with flowers like small white umbrellas. The horse scrambled down a steep limestone slope through slender silver birch trees. Isabel heard the hum of a working quarry nearby.

Suddenly a figure lurched in front of her, a man with red hair and a fiery beard. He grinned up at her, flashing a gold tooth, and grabbed her bridle. His nose was round and red, his eyes deep amber under thick red brows, and his breath had more than a hint of brandy. A gold hoop glittered in his ear. He removed his shabby tricorn hat.

'Good morrow. I saw ye riding this way on a fine hoss. I seem to have lost me way again, not been in these parts awhile. It would be kind indeed if you'd lend me a ride o' yer hoss, for the King's Revenue men lurk in these parts.'

'Captain Red Pete!' gasped Isabel.

'Indeed I am. An' many a song is sung 'ere on th' Isle 'bout me an' me crew.' He looked around. 'I don't like the feel o' this place. Filled wi' sounds of demons. Listen to them great beasts diggin' the land.'

'Those are machines working in the quarry,' explained Isabel.

'It's ungodly, all that roarin'. Mr Pearce, who runs His Majesty's quarries here on th' Isle, is a man o' learnin'. He's no call for monsters in 'is quarries with vast wheels an' silver teeth,' reflected Red Pete. 'Never mind, I've found me a place to stay with a fullsome lady while me ship's lost. At a white house near the Mermaid Inn.' He grabbed Isabel's arm and dragged her down from the horse. 'Yer one of them Maydew lasses, I reckon. Big grey eyes an' a high falutin' way o' speakin'.'

'I'm Isabel Maydew,' she said, shaking him off. 'I have to take my horse back to the farm, where he belongs.' As if in agreement, Isaac stamped on the pirate's toe.

'Ouch!' He hopped away from her. 'I could never get the hang o' hosses. A ship's a kinder beast by far. Look out for me cabin boy, Tom, wanderin' the Isle. I lost 'im in a storm, God help us, an' nothin's gone right since. We 'ave to leave this place o' weird magic, soon as we can.'

Quickly Isabel climbed on to Isaac and tugged at the reins, keen to return the horse safely to Groves stables. With a last glance over her shoulder at the pirate, she left Red Pete in the middle of the glade.

'Farewell,' he called after her. 'Tell Tom to return to the *Fortune*. He'll show up, bad penny that he is.'

'I'll tell him,' called Isabel.

'An' we'll meet again, Miss Maydew. I know it!'

'He's a very charming man,' declared Mrs Greychurch. 'My new friend, Captain Peter, takes a lot of interest in my antiques.' Mrs Greychurch dusted a Victorian glass vase gently with a large yellow cloth.

'Wraaff!' Gregor bounced around her, his tail brushing the vase. Mrs Groves leaped from the sofa and caught it as it toppled. She glared at Gregor, who slunk behind the sofa. Luckily, Mrs Greychurch had moved on to dusting the fireplace and had missed the incident.

'He's the captain of a ship, you know. Funny, I thought he was a pirate when we first met. How silly of me.' Mrs Greychurch gave a twinkling laugh.

Miranda stopped fiddling in the mirror with her false eyelashes. She put her hands on her hips, her face pink. 'He's emptying our drinks cabinet. I don't trust him. And he *is* eyeing our antiques.

I bet he makes off with them when you're down at the beach hut. What's the point of having a *Pirate Watch* if you invite pirates to stay in our house?'

Mrs Greychurch dusted the mantelpiece. 'I'm expecting Peter for lunch later, so be polite.'

Miranda headed for the door. 'I'm going to Weymouth to play Pirate Golf.'

'Again?' said Mrs Greychurch, but Miranda had already gone, slamming the door behind her. 'Still, at least she's out in the fresh air. I can't stand it when she hangs around in her room all day.' She looked at Mrs Groves. 'You look a lot better. Very nice of Flintlock to come and help out.'

'Yes, very nice,' said Mrs Groves cagily. Gregor had edged behind the sofa and was chewing something. She didn't want to look, but she suspected it was the fresh lilies from the hallway. Gregor had a taste for flowers during hot weather. They were cool and refreshing and he liked to crunch them up.

'Is Gregor all right?'

'Grrrp,' gulped Gregor from behind the sofa.

'He's fine, just resting I think,' said Mrs Groves. 'I've found him a personal trainer. They're all the rage nowadays. Ryder's offered to take him on.'

'Well, I hope he changes his shorts, they're enough to distract anyone,' said Mrs Greychurch.

'I'd like the *Free Portland News* to run a photo of Gregor at a Dog Agility Show,' Mrs Groves continued unperturbed. Gregor edged out from behind the sofa and looked accusingly at her. Bits of green stem stuck to his teeth and white petals clung to his nose. Mrs Groves whipped out a hanky and cleaned his face quickly. She looked behind the sofa where a sticky pile of flowers lay. 'I'd better take him home,' she said nervously, producing his lead. Gregor's eyebrows twitched. He raced across the room and dived behind the curtains, his bushy tail still showing.

'You silly dog,' said Mrs Groves. Gregor hadn't got the hang of hiding.

'Collies are supposed to be very clever,' reflected Mrs Greychurch. From a drawer, she took out her silver napkin holders engraved with tiny angels and laid them in a row, ready to polish, marvelling at how they gleamed in the sunlight. No wonder pirates risked their lives for treasure, she thought. After all, what was more alluring than silver and gold?

Mrs Groves reached behind the curtain and clipped the lead on Gregor's collar. He rolled his eyes sulkily as she led him across the room.

'Come on, boy, let's go home.'

'Brrrp,' he said, spitting out a petal.

After they had left, Mrs Greychurch switched on the radio to listen with growing horror to the news report on *Portland FM*. 'Pirates caused havoc this afternoon in Fortuneswell. The pirates, who all claim to be from a ship called the *Fortune*, waved swords at a shop keeper, stole pasties and sang sea shanties to an elderly lady. Reports of the marauding pirates have also come from Chiswell and Castletown, where the Port Inn was ransacked. The pirates were last seen leaving the fish and chip shop to climb on a bus to Easton.'

CHAPTER NINE

THE LOST *FORTUNE*

'Isabel, can you pop round to Penfold Lucke in Weston Street and collect some eggs for the cake?' asked Mrs Maydew, bustling around with her hair in large pink curlers. 'I start work at the Post Office at 1 o'clock and I don't have time to go myself.'

The climber Alfie and his friend Ryder sat at the kitchen table, eating sausages, fried tomatoes and toast. Ryder had Gregor at his feet, where he was chewing on a slobbery rope.

'I wanna go out,' whined Suzie. 'I'm bored an' I love them brown chicken hens. Why can't I go?'

'Sit,' commanded Ryder. 'Come on, dog dude, I promised I'd train you.' He pressed Gregor's tail. Gregor nipped him. 'Yeow!'

Suzie smacked Ryder. 'He doesn't like surfers! I'm trainin' him anyway. Siitt, Blackbeard!' Gregor sat down promptly and panted up at Suzie. 'Good dog,' she said, patting his head.

Ryder raised his bushy eyebrows and turned back to Alfie. 'I think we should tackle the *Long John Silver* climb near Cheyne Weares. I've got the hang of this climbing lark now.'

Alfie nodded, crunching toast. 'OK'.

Isabel sat opposite them, her chin in her hands, watching a line of wispy clouds float across the sky. In the distance, a tiny red crabbing boat bobbed on the sea. She was thinking about Red Pete, the notorious pirate captain. He seemed less scary than she had imagined. In fact, he was the sort of person she would like to talk to for hours; he would probably tell fantastic stories, but some of them would be true. And he seemed worried about Tom Lucke, his cabin boy.

'Isabel?' repeated her mother. 'Eggs?'

'I'm just going,' said Isabel, rising to her feet.

'Ready!' shouted Suzie. She had changed into her pirate costume and packed up Groover the cat in his basket, cramming a white bonnet on his head. 'It's his sun hat,' she explained.

'Come on then,' said Isabel reluctantly.

They took a route called the Giant's Footpath across the island, thick with brambles and tall nettles. Horses grazed in fields alongside the path and the Portland sheep wandered sleepily in the heat of the sun. With Suzie jogging beside her, Isabel headed for Weston Street and a row of cottages set in ramshackle gardens. She pushed back the gate to Lucke Cottage, wondering how the cottage had looked when Tom Lucke had lived there with his cousin, hundreds of years before. The path to Penfold's cottage was overgrown with summer flowers. Billowing lilies, pink and purple hydrangeas and pale yellow chrysanthemums wilted along the path. Ivy curled in long tendrils around the windows of the cottage.

The budgie swooped down to greet them, landing on Suzie's shoulder with a thump. She stroked his head gently and it preened against her hand, chattering loudly.

'He's a pirate budgie,' Suzie exclaimed. 'He likes me, I can tell.' The budgie tilted his head.

Isabel rapped on the door and the budgie flapped to the top of the apple tree.

Penfold greeted them wearing a flowery Hawaiian shirt. 'Hello, dears, come in. Have you called for eggs for the huge birthday cake?'

'Hello, Mr Lucke. You look silly,' said Suzie, staring at him. Isabel poked her.

'This is my best holiday shirt. What a nice cat. He's wearing a lovely hat, very stylish. Shall I re-tie the bow?' asked Penfold, peering into the basket.

'I rescued 'im,' said Suzie.

Groover miaowed. He jumped out of the basket and rubbed against Penfold's legs. Penfold patted him and the cat leaped on the kitchen table, purring loudly. He knocked over a book, *Ships of the 17th Century*. Isabel picked it up and glanced at a Dutch galleon. She turned the pages to an elegant ship with three tall masts and a mermaid figurehead. She studied the picture, remembering hanging on to the main mast of this ship in the storm and watching the cabin boy slide away from her across the deck. If Tom Lucke and Red Pete were wandering the island, she felt certain that this very ship *must* be anchored nearby.

Penfold looked at her curiously. He tapped the picture. 'That's the *Fortune*, a ship sailed by Portland pirates.'

'I'm a pirate too!' yelled Suzie.

'I'm going to write the story of this amazing ship and its adventures. I'll be famous,' explained Penfold. 'I expect you've read the reports of pirates in the *Echo*. Perhaps even seen the ship yourself?' He watched Isabel carefully.

'I've read about the ship,' she muttered.

Suzie glared at them both. 'Can we see them chickens now?' She pushed open the kitchen door, tugging Penfold with her.

'Riaow,' said Groover, trotting after Penfold.

'He likes you,' said Suzie to Penfold. 'You can 'ave him if you like.'

Outside, Tom Lucke pushed the leaves of the apple tree aside to see through the kitchen window, the budgie perched on his shoulder. He stroked the bird's head while he watched Isabel studying the book. The budgie chattered in his ear. The girl had stowed away on the *Fortune*. She must be a witch. Her magic may even have brought him here. Now he was stranded. He decided to stay close to Isabel. He lifted the bird from his shoulder, perched him on a twig and slid down from the tree.

Purple clouds gathered over the sea in a frowning line as evening drew in. Cottages gleamed in the drizzle of summer rain and the lost pirates of Portland's past left footprints in the mud, heading back to the Lucke Cottage after an exciting day. To the east of the Isle, Miranda sauntered along with her umbrella, hopping around puddles near her home at Church Ope. She spotted Isabel further along the road, rushing past the Portland Museum.

Miranda followed her, sneaking along a slippery path that wound through the trees to the cove, pausing every few steps to press her back against a tree and peer ahead, looking for Isabel. The tall oaks and chestnut trees caught the rain on rustling leaves. Thunder growled over the sea. Miranda snuffled and wiped her nose. She tiptoed under a stone archway into the church ruins and darted behind a large table-shaped grave. No sign of Isabel.

An owl hooted from a deep hole in a tree. Miranda jumped. 'Shhh!' Rain pattered on the leaves around her, like tapping fingers. She ran her hand along the mossy surface of the grave, where a grim skull and crossbones marked the stone. 'Creepy old pirates,' she said. She pushed the heavy lid of the grave. 'Bet it's full of treasure.' Miranda froze. She thought she heard someone breathe nearby.

Abandoning the graveyard she sped down the narrow, twisting steps to the beach. 'Eeeeek!' She slipped on the wet ground and landed with a thump. A figure loomed over her, his eyes glittering, a blue scarf wound around his head. Miranda heard the hiss of a sword being unsheathed. She shrieked again.

'Miranda, shut up,' cried Isabel, dashing through beach huts to her side.

Miranda clutched her arm. 'A man with a sword threatened me. A pirate!'

'Are you sure? I didn't see anyone.' Isabel looked into the growing darkness, the only sound the hushing of waves on the shore. The beach was full of lurking shadows.

'Of course I'm sure. Why are you creeping around here anyway?' snapped Miranda.

Isabel sat back on her heels. 'You're following me again.'

'Maybe,' admitted Miranda, struggling to her feet. In the pale summer twilight, she could just make out a figure on the shore.

'Over there! It's Flintlock,' breathed Miranda. 'Are we spying on him?'

'Don't be ridiculous,' exclaimed Isabel.

'Let's follow him,' said Miranda eagerly. She shoved Isabel ahead of her. 'If we climb up the steps to Rufus Castle we can work our way around the edge of the cove and close in on him. You go first. Keep a look out for pirates.'

Behind the beach hut, Tom Lucke held Cutlass in a tight grip, his arm linked around the pirate's throat. 'I can't breathe, ye little fool,' snarled Cutlass, struggling.

'That witch Isabel may be our only chance o' findin' our way back to the ship. We're lost in this strange place wi' metal horses and all kinds o' weird beasts. You're the fool round 'ere, Cutlass. You could have harmed 'er, wavin' that sword around.' He pushed Cutlass away from him.

'Since when d'ye give me orders? I'm the ship's carpenter. Yer nothin' but a nobody. Just a pair o' hands,' sneered Cutlass.

Tom turned away. 'I'm not listenin' to you no more, Cutlass. And I'm not comin' back to the *Fortune* to skivvy day an' night. Leave me be.' He stalked away into the darkness.

Just north of the cove, Isabel and Miranda crept along the eastern shore protected by a line of large rocks. They crouched behind the boulders and peered over. The waves lapped in shallow pools around their feet.

'Can you see any eels?' asked Miranda nervously, swishing her feet in the water.

'Not at the moment. Flintlock's over there, looking out to sea,' whispered Isabel.

'You find conger eels here sometimes,' said Miranda, 'not to mention crabs, cuttlefish, dogfish and shrimps. Even sea cucumbers can attack you.'

'I heard something. Did you hear it?' asked Isabel.

'Nope,' said Miranda, hopping from one foot to the other.

Isabel studied Flintlock. The waves rolled in towards the beach, splashing gently around their feet.

'He'ss searching for a pirate sship.'

'Could be,' said Isabel. 'D'you reckon that's a lantern he's holding?'

'Perhapss he lookss for a ssignal.'

'Why are you talking funny?' asked Miranda. She blew her nose.

'I'm not,' said Isabel, gazing out to sea. 'I think you're right, he's looking for a signal.'

'Why am I right? The signal thing was your idea,' said Miranda. They looked at each other blankly.

'Ssslow-witted girlss,' said the mermaid, resting her elbows lightly on the rock next to them.

Miranda fell backwards into the sea. 'Ahhh!' she shrieked, paddling her arms frantically. 'Don't touch me! I thought my mother harpooned you!'

The mermaid hissed.

Miranda scrambled to her feet and sloshed towards the shore. 'Hit her with something!' she yelled to Isabel. 'She wants me to be a mermaid but I've gone off the idea. Tell her you'll do it. No one'll miss you.'

'Sshame,' said the mermaid, 'she'd have made a good mermaid in ssome wayss. She's ruthlesss.'

'I'm going home. I know *you* like hanging around with eels, mermaids and evil old pirates, but I've had enough,' called Miranda, vanishing into the bushes. Isabel and the mermaid looked at one another. The tide was coming in, the choppy waves lapping around them. Soon the rocks would be cut off by the sea. The mermaid smiled, showing sharp teeth.

Isabel backed against a rock, as far from the mermaid as possible. 'What d'you want?' she asked.

'My dear friend, Issabel Maydew, thiss is all your fault. You called the pirates across the seas of time. Meddling again with the ancient magic of the Isle.'

'I didn't bring them here,' said Isabel angrily. '*You* called them! And you've hidden their ship! Where are the other pirates?'

The mermaid studied her long fingernails. 'Red Pete hass defied me for the lasst time. Ssoon he will beg for my help. Perhapss I'll rid myself of him once and for all.' She lunged at Isabel, who jumped away.

'I was expecting that, mermaid.'

The mermaid splashed her tail in the sea, soaking Isabel from head to foot. 'Maybe sso,' she murmured. She leaned forward, fixing Isabel with an hypnotic stare. 'If you give me the secretss of time, you'll be free of the passt and I'll ssend the pirates back to where they belong.'

Isabel shook her head. 'I don't have any secrets to give.'

The mermaid's eyes glowed an eerie green. 'If I could hold time in my handss, what power that would be! What magic! Better than conjuring storms from the sea,' she said, her long fingers clawing the air. 'Even better than weaving dreams for sleeperss on the Isle.'

'You sent that terrible sea storm?' gasped Isabel, '*and* my dreams about the *Fortune*?'

'Of course, it wass easy. *Time* iss the greatest magic.' The mermaid ran her fingers through her red hair, flicking drops of sea water at Isabel. 'My friend Tom Lucke hass a great destiny, but it's sslipping through his fingers. Luckily I'm here to guide him,' she said with a sinister smile.

The mermaid stretched up her slender white arms, arched her back and, with a final glance at Isabel, flipped into a dive.

Isabel scrambled across the rocks, turning briefly to see the mermaid swim out to sea. 'Her friend, Tom,' she repeated to herself. Had the mermaid enchanted Tom to exact revenge on Red Pete? She shivered. Any friend of the infamous Siren was someone to watch out for. She had to find the cabin boy again and discover what he and the mermaid were planning.

A light flickered over Isabel. Flintlock held up his lantern and studied the girl. Her eyes were as grey as the stones of Church Ope beach, he thought. 'Out wanderin' by yerself? Is this Maydew witch business?'

'I'm not a witch,' said Isabel.

Flintlock shrugged. 'A bit o' witchin's no bad thing. Some folk rate it highly. Your family help many with their healing herbs. Miss Maydew teaches the little children o' the Isle at her schoolhouse. Yet folk will always remember Agnes, the first Maydew witch, an' fear the Maydews, whatever good they do.'

Flintlock rubbed his brow, staring out to sea. 'Thought I saw the *Fortune*. One moment t'were there, then gone.' He frowned. 'Take care here tonight. There are strange things afoot i' Church Ope, an ancient place. Vikings named it *Ope* when they pirated these shores, dragging their fearsome longboats out o' the sea. Now Red Pete's sailed the *Fortune* to Portland. I never thought he'd return. Pirates, all of 'em, with a love o' the sea and the sword.'

Isabel hesitated. 'I'm looking for Red Pete's cabin boy, Tom Lucke.'

Flintlock stopped, his eyes glinting. 'D'ye know who he is, Miss Maydew?'

Isabel shuddered, thinking of the mermaid and her claims to the cabin boy.

Flintlock continued. 'He's a restless boy from an ole island family. Watched over by the Siren, the legendary mermaid. Best if he returns to his ship. I'm certain the *Fortune*'s anchored near here, full to the brim with precious cargo from French 'n' Spanish ships.'

'Pirate treasure,' said Isabel.

'Of course, the ship's overladen,' said Flintlock. 'That must be why Red Pete put in to the Isle durin' the storm. Why else would he anchor here after so long? Then I know exactly where he's hidden his ill-gotten gains; his silver and gold, jewels an' spices.'

'You plan to find his treasure and steal it?' accused Isabel.

'Perhaps,' pondered Flintlock, folding his arms. 'In any case, let's leave this place to the ghosts of Viking warriors. I'll walk you to

Wakeham. You can make your way home from there. Steer clear of Tom Lucke. One day he'll be a very dangerous Portland pirate.'

An owl, like a small white spirit, soared over them and flew across the oak trees that circled the bay. Isabel watched it fly as she followed Flintlock up the beach, wondering whether it was true that the cabin boy was destined to be a villainous pirate.

CHAPTER TEN

TREASURE TROVE

Gregor pushed open the bedroom door with his nose and leaped on Mrs Groves' bed. 'Woomff, Gregor!' she gasped. He whined at her, his eyes shiny in the darkness. 'What's the matter with you?' He scrabbled with his paws until he found a comfortable place in the crook of her knee and curled up, sighing.

Moonlight trickled between the curtains from a moon as gold as a glittering coin. Too hot to sleep, Mrs Groves threw back the covers and sat up. She heard a door slam. Slipping out of bed, she peered from the window. A boy was walking across the yard, heading for the stables, eating a loaf of bread. Puzzled, she decided to follow him. She tiptoed from the bedroom to the stairs, holding her breath as the wooden stairs creaked. A row of pictures lined the staircase: cannons at Portland Castle; a black dog chasing a troop of Civil War soldiers. Mrs Groves looked at the last picture, a watercolour of two boys playing in the farmyard. She always wondered who the boys were. The scent of wallflowers drifted through the farmhouse from open windows overlooking the garden. From the apple trees in the small farm orchard, she heard the lilting song of a nightingale.

Mrs Groves walked quietly to the lounge where Flintlock was sleeping on the sofa, breathing deeply. He turned in his sleep and murmured to himself. The grandfather clock ticked slowly in the corner. She gasped in amazement. Around him were piles of gold sovereigns, silver candlesticks, goblets and dishes set with precious stones. 'Extraordinary!' she breathed.

She slipped out of the room and walked lightly to the stables. As she suspected, the boy was stretched out on bales of straw, fast asleep, a half-eaten loaf in his hand. She noticed a dark tattoo of a ship's wheel on his arm. Mrs Groves found a woollen horse blanket and draped it over the sleeping boy.

Returning to the farmhouse, she sank into an old flowery armchair in the lounge and looked with a mixture of dismay and fascination at the sparkling array of treasure. She decided to wait for Flintlock to wake up. She looked at a cup inlaid with blood-red rubies. Carefully she replaced it and lifted a chain with an emerald as large as a dragon's eye. For just a second she closed her eyes. The chain slipped from her fingers as she drifted asleep, dreaming of a dragon in a small cave.

'We'll have the farm back in shape before you know it, Aunt Estelle.'

Mrs Groves woke with a start to find that the treasure had disappeared and Flintlock was in the kitchen, repairing a cupboard with Gregor close by his side, chewing a hammer.

'Look at this lazy dog. He can follow me out on a ride this morning.' Gregor shook his fur out into a black and white cloud. 'Pay the bills, there's coins enough here, an' more to spend as ye wish.' Flintlock dropped a handful of gold sovereigns on the kitchen table. Mrs Groves tottered to her feet and picked one up. Solid gold and hundreds of years old.

'Are these yours, Flintlock?' she asked hesitantly.

Flintlock scratched the back of his neck. 'Finder's keepers. Come now, Gregor, 'tis a fine day. Let us head up to yonder Verne. We can look at the ships and King Henry's fine ole castle.'

Mrs Groves waited until Flintlock and Gregor had gone. She peered behind the sofa and opened the door to the grandfather clock. No sign of any treasure. Briefly, she wondered if she should tell her friend, Mrs Greychurch. After all, the treasure was clearly stolen. The clock chimed. It was time to see to the horses. She also wanted to talk to the boy, who was sleeping in the stables and stealing food from the kitchen. She headed outside again, crossing the yard to the stable, where she found a neatly folded blanket in the corner. The mysterious boy had vanished.

Daylight crept into the small bedroom of Lucke Cottage on Weston Street. Sparrows twittered in the ivy growing around the windows. After a humid night, Penfold Lucke was leaning by the open window in a long stripy nightshirt, his chin in his hand. Groover the cat stretched on the windowsill next to him. Penfold stroked him absentmindedly. Isabel was hiding something, he was sure of it. He had seen how carefully she had studied the picture of the *Fortune*. He would have to keep a close eye on Isabel Maydew.

The curtains blew around him in warm gusts like a sail on a ship. A tiny round wren hopped along a branch of the pear tree below him and disappeared into bushes. The budgie fluttered to his side and tilted its head at Penfold. 'I'll feed you later,' he said. He gazed south towards the hazy blue-grey sea. The clomp of heavy boots startled him. Three ramshackle men were walking along the road. Groover miaowed and jumped down from the window.

Penfold gaped at them. They loitered by the cottage, one of them resting his arm on the gate, making it swing, as he swigged from a bottle. Penfold breathed in sharply and listened.

'Red Pete's very last word to ye was to stay aboard the *Fortune*. Keep watch, while 'e searched for tha' young varmint Tom an' stowed goods ashore,' insisted a short pirate in a baggy black waistcoat over a stripy shirt.

'He's been gone awhile, Shorty. Two days an' nights. The rest o' the crew 'ave been at the Inn, singin' and shoutin'. Niver fear. Mr Otter's still aboard.'

'We'll 'ave more o' them hot potatoes later, chopped to bits an' boiled in oil, from the cook in Fortuneswell,' said Bill, a tall pirate with a patch over one eye, wearing a long, tattered coat.

Just then Mr Otter appeared at the gate and joined the other pirates. 'What're ye doin' a wanderin', Boatswain Bill? I thought ye was with yon ship.'

Bill sniffed. 'Nay, but 'tis fine for *you* to waddle around the Isle, Mr Otter, Ship's Cook.'

'Who's guardin' the *Fortune* then an' all its fine goods and chattels?' asked Mr Otter, jowls wobbling, his thick eyebrows rising like two alarmed caterpillars.

Shorty shrugged. 'No-one, I reckons. The *Fortune's* safe enough anchored by the Weares. Who would board a *pirate* ship full o' cannon? Where've ye been, Mr Otter?'

'Stockin' up on foodstuff. A shinin' market full o' food in Easton village 'ad plenty to spare. Flashed the blade o' me dagger an' gorrus meat 'n' bread. Look ee here, 'tis Cutlass.'

Another pirate, with fishy eyes and a blue scarf wrapped around his head, appeared by the gate. He pushed Bill aside to question Shorty. 'I've tramped over field an' wood, here an' there, an' no sign of our ship. Where's the *Fortune* gone, Quarter Master?'

Shorty looked guilty, shuffling his feet. 'We ain't been back to the ship fer a day or so. Been busy a'piratin' the Isle.'

''Tis gone, you fools! Vanished!' shouted Cutlass. 'Red Pete's taken the best of our haul o' treasure and gorn with never a word to us, norra please nor thank ee.'

'No sign o' Red Pete, and we've bin all over the Isle,' said Shorty, shaking his head. 'We've seen 'orrible grey ships down Castletown an' roarin' horses what carry folk faster'n arrows from Underhill to Top.'

'Ahoy!' A young pirate appeared from the road. 'The *Fortune's* gone! We went back to the ship after a nice quiet evenin' with a noggin' o' rum at the Inn, and no sign at all.'

'Bleet, where's Tom Lucke? Is he swimmin' around with that comely sea nymph, what strikes fear o' god into Red Pete?' asked Bill.

'Aye, I've seen Tom,' interrupted Cutlass. 'He's stoppin' ashore.

Had enough o' piratin'. Red Pete should niver have brung 'im aboard. The lad asks too many cliver questions. He's full of what little ee knows 'bout nothin'.'

'The gold's mine,' squawked the budgie by Penfold's elbow. The pirates turned and stared at him. Shorty politely removed his hat.

'Good morn t'ee. We're seekin' Red Pete, good sire.'

'Are you pirate ghosts?' asked Penfold. There was muffled laughter and shuffling, as the men considered this.

'Aye, ghosts lookin' for a lost soul.'

'Oh,' said Penfold. He took in their shabby grey trousers, long shirts and leather boots.

''Ave you seen 'im?' asked Shorty.

'No,' said Penfold, 'but I'd like to find him. He's captain of the *Fortune*, I believe.'

Cutlass drew his sword. 'What d'ye know 'bout it?'

Shorty nudged him in the ribs. 'Hush, let 'im be. Everyone knows Red Pete round here.'

Penfold squinted at the dark tattoo on Cutlass's forearm, shaped like a wheel.

Shorty stepped forward, pushing back the gate. He stood beneath Penfold's window. Under dark brows, his eyes glowed with a pale light like the moon on a summer evening. 'I go by the name o' Shorty, good sire, ship's Quarter Master, and ye be ...?'

'Penfold Lucke.' He heard the pirate's sharp intake of breath.

Bill grabbed Shorty's sleeve and pulled him away, whispering in his ear, 'No point askin' him about Red Pete. He looks daft as a cowcumber.'

Cutlass pointed a sword at Penfold. 'No word o' this! I'll come back 'nother day.'

As they wandered away along Weston Street, Bill sang, 'Ye must make me a fine Holland shirt, Blow, blow, blow, ye winds, blow.'

Penfold sank on to his pine bed, watching the curtain billow in the sea breeze. The budgie edged along the windowsill and peered in at him. 'The gold's mine!' he squawked again. Startled, Groover leaped on to the bed and hid under a pillow.

'Pirates from the *Fortune*,' Penfold whispered. He grabbed a pen and notepad and started to scribble. 'This is my chance. A true story, told by the captain himself. Villainous Red Pete. I must find him. Tomorrow I'll follow Isabel. She knows where the ship's anchored, I'm sure of it. She's keeping secrets.'

'Riaow,' said Groover, peering from under the pillow.

CHAPTER ELEVEN

SWIFT AS A SHADOW

Isabel and Suzie sat in the cool shade of Groves oak tree watching the surfer Ryder gambol across the field, wearing a short-sleeved summer wetsuit with orange stripes and big flip-flops. His climbing helmet was crammed over his fluffy hair. He lined up a row of surfboards for Gregor to jump. Mrs Groves set up a picnic table with glasses of juice and sandwiches. She placed an old straw sunhat on her head to keep off the sun. Mrs Greychurch, in a vivid pink sundress decorated with green crocodiles, was arranging a vase of sunflowers on the table. Two pied wagtails hopped nearby in the sunshine, eating crumbs.

Suzie picked a handful of white daisies and looped them in a chain around her pirate sword. She jumped as Ryder shot in front of her, leaping the surfboards.

'Stop him! He's squashing my daisies,' yelled Suzie at Isabel, who was gazing up into the oak tree. The edges of the leaves were painted gold with sunlight, making her eyes ache. She had got up just after dawn and trailed from one end of the Isle to the other, looking for Tom. No sign of the cabin boy, although she had the uneasy feeling that she was being followed.

'Run! Jump! Up! Over we go,' Ryder shouted at Gregor. He reached the last surfboard and punched the air. 'Yeah, we did it!' Gregor was still lying in the middle of the field, his tongue lolling from his mouth. 'Go round again, keep moving,' yelled Ryder, running wildly in a circle. Gregor rose to his feet and ambled behind him. 'Fetch!' bawled Ryder, throwing a snorkel. Gregor wandered over and sniffed it. He lay flat on his stomach with the snorkel and chewed it, rolling his eyes at Ryder, who was still running around the field.

'What're we doing next?' demanded Suzie, putting a daisy chain around her neck.

Isabel sighed and leaned back against the trunk of the oak, closing her eyes. 'I need to find a cabin boy from a ship called the *Fortune*, and you have to go home to help with the cake.'

'Yes!' exclaimed Suzie, licking her lips. 'I'm in charge of icing!'

Penfold appeared suddenly from behind the tree, with Groover the cat draped over his shoulder. 'The *Fortune*?' he repeated.

Suzie leaped to her feet and grabbed Penfold by the sleeve, pulling a notebook from her pirate hat. 'Mr Lucke, d'you like ownin' Groover? It's for my web page.'

Penfold considered this. 'Well, of course, I'm very proud. Being a cat owner is an important job. When I go back to work at the library, I'll do a book display about cats.' He looked around and scowled. Isabel had disappeared.

Red Pete sneaked through the ruins of St Andrew's Church to the old graveyard, where he gazed across the mirror-like sea, looking for his ship. Gulls swooped over the water, their curved wings scything the air. He traced his finger over a faded angel wing on an old gravestone. Perhaps the guns fired from the Spanish city of Cadiz had hit their mark and he was an angel now too. A slow worm with golden eyes slithered across the dry ground towards his boots. He moved to let the creature pass.

'Swift as a shadow,' he said, looking around at the old gravestones. 'One minute yer alive, fightin' and drinkin', then yer an angel.' He scratched his head. 'I feel 'xactly the same as when I was a pirate cap'n.'

White clouds billowed over the sea. He squinted into the sky. 'That's a sail in the heavens. A ship's bow atop o' that cloud. An' a mermaid figurehead! My very ship! This is old island magic!'

Unsheathing his sword, he ran down the narrow steps to the bay. 'Where are you, meddling sea witch?' he bellowed. Waves rolled gently towards the shore and a mist drifted like smoke across the sea. A high, thin voice was singing. 'Mermaid!' he cried, running into the shallow waves, waving his sword in a loop over his head.

Red Pete stopped. As the mist slid by, touching him like clammy hands, he saw a pale, slender girl with a long turquoise tail, perched on a rock that jutted into the sea.

'What d'you sseek, Pirate Captain Red Pete?'

He plunged through the waves, the water splashing above his boots. He stopped an arm's length from the mermaid, pointing the sword at her throat. She blinked her glowing green eyes but did not flinch. 'You follow my ship too closely, mermaid. I know your scheming ways! Where's the *Fortune*?'

The mermaid leaned back to evade the point of the silver sword. She pushed the weapon aside with one long finger. 'I don't know where your ship restss. Perhapss on the sea bed, where fishes swim among the tall mastss. The witch Issabel Maydew brought you here. Not my doing. Only sshe can find your sship for you.'

'That young Maydew girl wi' gentle grey eyes? The girl means no harm to anyone. She'd climb yonder cliffs to fetch a butterfly in peril.' He laughed bitterly. 'Look at me, Siren o' the Portland seas. No ship to command, no sign o' Tom or the rest o' me crew. Who am I, if not captain o' the *Fortune*?'

'A nobody, I ssuppose,' smiled the mermaid coldly.

Red Pete gritted his teeth and swung the sword through the air with a whoosh. The mermaid twisted away. He shook his fist at her. 'Be off, vile Siren.'

The mermaid slithered into the sea, her blood-red hair pooling around her as she slid beneath the water, her eyes glittering.

'Soon as I find my ship, I'll be lookin' for you, sea witch!'

The mermaid disappeared, leaving the surface of the sea as smooth as a mirror. Red Pete stared across the calm water. The stillness worried him. He shivered. Suddenly the mermaid lunged from the waves, so close that he could see drops of water glittering like diamonds across her pale cheeks and the flash of green in her eyes. She wrenched the sword from his hand and dived beneath the sea with a flick of her powerful tail, leaving the pirate captain unarmed.

Miranda Greychurch leaned against the cliffs by Cheyne Weares, a yellow sunhat crammed on her head. She rummaged in her rucksack for an apple. 'Aachoo.' She muffled the sneeze in her tissue and mopped her nose. Looking up, she watched Peggy scale the top of a cliff, attaching her harness clip on to bolts in the rock. Fluffy white clouds drifted across the sky like lost Portland sheep. Miranda enjoyed the cooling sea breeze against her face. She heard a flapping sound, like the wings of a giant gull. Huge creamy sails rose from a cloud and a white ship sailed towards her. Miranda blinked in amazement.

'Hello, maid,' called a voice behind her. The ship melted into the sky.

Miranda jumped, dropping her apple. A boy leaned on a rock nearby. She took in his ragged clothes, his thin arms and eyes that were too old for his face. His hair fell across his brow. 'I 'spose the pirate look's in this summer,' she sniffed. 'What d'you want?'

Tom narrowed his eyes. 'Are ye a witch?'

'Don't be cheeky,' sniffed Miranda. She opened her bag. The boy watched her hungrily. 'Get your own picnic,' she snapped. The boy shrugged and looked out to sea. Miranda relented. 'Want one?' she asked, offering him an apple. The boy shook his head. As she crunched, Miranda noticed his hair glowing in the sunlight like a new copper coin. Every now and then, the air around him sparkled. Miranda's fingers tingled with an urge to poke the boy. 'My name's Miranda, by the way, not maid, and I have to go home in a minute and keep an eye on an awful pirate with red hair who's staying with my mother.'

'Red Pete!' exclaimed the boy, 'a man not much taller 'n me, red hair an' a gold tooth?'

'That's him,' said Miranda.

The boy looked thoughtful. 'Is 'e shoutin' an' hollerin' for me?'

Miranda stuffed her half-eaten apple in her bag. 'You can ask him yourself.' She started off along the zigzag path around the rocks. 'Follow me!' she yelled over her shoulder.

Tom hesitated, reluctant to face the pirate captain. He looked down at the clear turquoise sea. With a tiny shimmer that sent ripples across the water, a face with emerald green eyes rose from the tranquil sea. The boy stared at the mermaid. Water trickled down her glowing pale cheeks, white and pure as a statue in a church. The boy crouched and reached out his hand to touch hair as red as the fragile poppies that bloomed in Portland fields. He ran a long strand through his fingers, fascinated. The mermaid smiled, revealing sharp teeth, and curled her long fingers around his arm. The boy shivered. Her hands were icy cold, the nails curved and blue.

'We're old friendss,' she said.

Tom knelt back on his heels. 'I remember,' he breathed, 'you saved me when I fell from the ship. Then you left me i' the Portland *Race* to swim for me life!'

'A short distance from land, brave Tom Lucke. D'you know *why* I ssaved you?' asked the mermaid, her fingers still curled tightly around his wrist like a strand of seaweed.

Tom shook his head.

The mermaid caught him at the back of his neck and pulled him closer. She whispered in his ear, 'You musst take the *Fortune* for yourself. Cutlass showed you how to use a ssword. Get rid of Red Pete. He'ss abandoned the ship, taken the finest treasure for himself. It'ss your destiny to avenge thiss.'

He shuddered. 'I often dream of you, mermaid. Sometimes I feel like a sea creature myself.'

'Perhapss you are. Your ancestor Ssally Lucke once promised me a child, to live with the people of the ssea. Ancient creatures, our fate is a lonely one. Thiss is your chance to be a great captain, my ssea urchin.'

From a narrow gap in the rocks, the mermaid drew a gleaming silver sword, the hilt set with four glittering rubies. She rested the sword across her arm, offering it to the boy. 'It'ss yours,' she said. 'Red Pete cast it away.'

Tom reached down slowly and took the dripping sword from her. The mermaid vanished with barely a splash of her tail. Tom set off after Miranda, carrying Red Pete's sword, his eyes almost as cold as the mermaid's.

CHAPTER TWELVE

A CANNON AT THE READY

Gregor slunk through a hedgerow and scuttled beneath the drooping pink roses in the farm garden. He slid through the back door of the farmhouse into the cool kitchen. There he sank on to the stone-paved floor with a sigh and stretched out with eyes closed. His stomach growled. He opened one eye, staggered to his feet and snuffled at the cupboards. With the tip of his nose he pushed open a door. He grabbed the edge of a bag of dog biscuits firmly between his teeth and tugged until it unravelled. The bag toppled and fell, scattering biscuits across the kitchen floor. Gregor followed the trail, munching loudly. He shook out his fur, sending slobber around the room. He tottered to his bed in the corner where he licked his paws, closed his eyes and fell asleep.

The kitchen door pushed open again. Mrs Groves put her hands on her hips and sighed. 'I turn my back for 5 minutes and look what this naughty dog gets up to, Isabel. Ryder's supposed to be training Gregor, but he's still running around the field on his own. He looks very warm in that wet-suit,' she commented. 'What did you say you were looking for?'

'A book about pirate ships,' said Isabel.

Mrs Groves raised her eyebrows. 'Well, you're welcome to look along the book shelves.' Mrs Groves grabbed the broom and swept biscuits across the kitchen floor while Isabel headed for the dining room. Gregor snored peacefully in his bed. Mrs Groves leaned on the broom and wiped her forehead. 'Look at the mess. I never sit down.' She put some cakes out on a plate and left them in the middle of the table. They would be gone by the evening. The mysterious boy was eating well.

In the dining room, Isabel ran her hand over a heavy green and gold book lying on the desk. She had lent it to Mrs Groves a few months ago. Mrs Groves had placed a bookmark about halfway, marking the *Southern Sea Dragon*. Isabel turned the pages and looked at a picture of a golden-green dragon with broad seaweed-like wings and yellow eyes. She smiled. She missed the sea dragon and the magic he had brought with him.

She pulled out a shabby book with gold lettering on the spine, *A History of Pirates*, and perched on a chair to read it. There was a small picture of the *Fortune*, 'the infamous Dorset Pirate ship, commanded by Captain Tom Lucke, famed for his exploits on both sides of the Channel.'

'The cabin boy!' gasped Isabel. 'He and the mermaid must be planning to commandeer the *Fortune*.' She sat up sharply, nearly dropping the heavy book. 'What'll become of Red Pete?'

She put the book back on the shelf and pushed the chair under the gleaming mahogany table. She heard Mrs Groves in the lounge. The familiar room was cool even in summer, with two low latticed windows overlooking a small garden where flowerbeds full of blowsy, old-fashioned pink and yellow roses bloomed. The sagging armchairs around the room were comfortable and usually scattered with newspapers, boiled sweet wrappers and chewed cushions.

Isabel stopped in the lounge doorway, stunned. The dusty old armchairs had been replaced by a plump green sofa. New pictures of farm collies and race horses adorned the walls. On the mahogany sideboard were silver candlesticks and wide china dishes. Stylish clocks ticked loudly around the room. Even the raspberry-pink curtains were brand new.

'Where's all the furniture gone?' asked Isabel.

'Ah,' said Mrs Groves guiltily, 'it's in the shed. It was getting old anyway.'

'But you like old things,' said Isabel.

'Of course, but it's time for a change. I'm just putting up some lovely photos of Gregor. Sweep out the old, in with the new!'

Mrs Groves poked her head out of the door. 'Gregor, I can hear you chewing. If you're in that kitchen cupboard again, I'll put you on a diet of white fish!' she shouted. Gregor trotted into the lounge. Bits of pink feather duster stuck out of his mouth. 'Oh no, he's found my duster. I can't keep anything nice. Get down from that sofa, Gregor. Stop it! There's fur all over those cushions now.' Gregor rolled on to his back on the sofa, wagging his tail. 'You naughty dog!'

Isabel picked up a gleaming gold coin from the rug and interrupted her. 'Where did this coin come from?'

'I've found a few antiques, jewels and coins. Don't look at me like that. It's not as if I'm a pirate!' said Mrs Groves, snatching the coin from Isabel and stuffing it in her pocket.

Mrs Greychurch dragged her cannon along the narrow road to Rufus Castle. If she pulled the cannon backwards, it was fairly easy to move. However, as the road narrowed to a winding path it became awkward to manoeuvre. Mrs Greychurch sat on the cannon to catch her breath.

'If I can just get round that corner over there, and through the arch below the castle, I can place the cannon overlooking the bay. Good heavens!' Mrs Greychurch shrieked as the cannon rolled down the slope away from her. It clumped into a stone wall near the archway, shaking the ruins. A rock ricocheted from the top of the Norman keep. Mrs Greychurch looked around guiltily. The sun beamed through the leafy sycamores. Luckily she was still alone. 'But I know there's a pirate ship out there somewhere,' she said to herself.

'Need a hand wi' that, Missus?'

Mrs Greychurch turned to see a short man in a stripy shirt and black waistcoat. She smoothed her hair. 'How kind. If you could just lift the end of the cannon, I could move it a little.'

Shorty lifted the cannon for her and turned it with an expert hand. He patted it before departing. 'Fine piece o' work.'

'I'm very proud of it,' preened Mrs Greychurch. She collided with Isabel and Ben as she reversed the cannon below Rufus Castle. 'Dear girl!' cried Mrs Greychurch, pouncing on Isabel and hugging her. 'You and I alone are waging war on pirates. Help me with this cannon.'

'What's it for, Mrs Greychurch?' Isabel asked nervously. She could feel Ben laughing silently behind her. Mrs Greychurch kept a firm grip on her sleeve and looked shiftily at Ben.

'For blasting pirate ships from the sea, of course,' she said.

Isabel was shocked. She looked at the crumbling walls of Rufus Castle. 'You shouldn't fire a cannon so near the ruins!'

'Don't be silly,' said Mrs Greychurch. 'Cannons are often fired from castles.'

'But perhaps not Rufus Castle, which is usually called Bow and Arrow Castle,' Ben chipped in.

'Yes, I know, built by William Rufus, a great Norman king, son of William the Conqueror,' interrupted Mrs Greychurch. 'It was also captured by Robert, Earl of Gloucester for the Empress Matilda, a very sensible lady, who I'm sure had a cannon or two of her own.' As they were talking, Mrs Greychurch had managed to place her cannon overlooking the bay at the viewpoint above Church Ope Cove.

Ben produced his iPhone and flicked it on. 'I've got a new history app.'

Mrs Greychurch rotated the gun and ignored him. 'Perfect,' she said, looking across the gleaming blue sea. She pushed Isabel aside to line up the cannon with the barrel pointing over the wall. 'I can get a good shot from up here.' She looked around hopefully. No sign of the ship. A little disappointed, she turned back to Isabel. 'Run and get the gunpowder from my wardrobe, dear.'

Ben made a snorting noise, trying not to laugh, and Isabel glared at him. 'I can't wait to see this,' he said. 'I'll stay with Mrs G.'

Mrs Greychurch leaned over Isabel, her breath warm against her face. 'Hurry up, dear. We need gunpowder.' She tapped the cannon.

'Gunpowder,' repeated Isabel.

'Of course, it won't fire without it. Honestly, what do they teach in schools nowadays?'

'We don't do cannons,' insisted Isabel.

Mrs Greychurch pushed Ben out of the way and sat on the gun, looking mistily into the distance. 'When I was a girl, we covered the Gunpowder Plot every November. I always made notes. I was a very keen pupil. Off you go. The key's under the mat.'

Glad to escape, Isabel ran along the path away from the curving bay of Church Ope. As she turned the corner near the Portland Museum, she collided with Penfold Lucke, who had been visiting the Museum shop.

'Isabel! I've been looking for you.' He gripped her shoulder. Groover the cat was draped across his arm, watching her with unblinking eyes. 'We just popped into the Museum. Groover doesn't like being left at home,' he explained.

'I know. Suzie took him out a lot, usually in his basket,' said Isabel.

'I heard you mention the *Fortune* yesterday,' said Penfold accusingly. 'I think you should tell me everything you know about Red Pete and the pirate ship. I'm writing a book about the Portland pirates. I've even met some pirates from the *Fortune*.'

'You've met the pirates!' exclaimed Isabel.

'Yes, and I plan to interview Captain Red Pete as well.' Seeing that Isabel recognised the name, he continued. 'So you know him, do you?' Penfold stroked Groover who purred loudly. He slipped on a pair of glasses linked around his neck on a chain and looked closely at Isabel, taking in her light grey eyes and curling brown hair. Groover miaowed. 'I have to go soon, it's Groover's lunchtime and he hates missing meals.' He hooked his arm through Isabel's. 'I'll walk to Easton with you.'

'But I'm busy,' insisted Isabel.

'We can talk about the *Fortune* on the way and you can tell me absolutely everything you know about Red Pete. My pirate story'll be a best-seller, I know it.'

Mrs Greychurch was looking at her watch. 'Where's Isabel got to?' she exclaimed. Ben shrugged. To make matters worse, her daughter Miranda was wandering up the path with a scruffy boy.

'For goodness sakes, Miranda, who's this?' she snapped.

'A friend of Peter's. Come on, Tom, I bet he's at home fingering the silver,' said Miranda.

'Does that boy have any proper clothes?' her mother demanded, looking at Tom's cut-off trousers and ripped shirt. 'And is that a sword? Why's he dressed like a pirate?'

'It's fashionable. You're always horrible to my friends,' bleated Miranda, pulling Tom along the path.

Mrs Greychurch sniffed. 'Fashion, humph.' She whipped a duster out of her trouser pocket and polished the cannon. 'Ben, you'll have to go and find Isabel. Tell her to hurry up.'

'OK,' he agreed. He was bored anyway. Despite himself, he found his eyes drawn to the sea. What if there really was a pirate ship anchored off the coast of Portland? He shoved his hands in his pockets and trudged after Miranda.

'A fine cannon you've got there,' remarked Red Pete, appearing from the cliff path winding below Rufus Castle. The breeze ruffled his fiery hair.

Mrs Greychurch jumped. 'Peter! A ship's flying the skull and crossbones out there, bold as anything. We have to fight piracy.'

'Is that so?' Red Pete gazed out to sea, searching the horizon for the *Fortune*.

'It's our duty,' said Mrs Greychurch sternly.

'Maybe pirates ain't as bad as ye think. Men go to sea to better themselves. I left the Isle many moons ago, took meself a fine ship, the *Fortune,* and found Portland lads to follow me.'

'So you *are* a pirate! Sailing the seven seas to capture treasure!' gasped Mrs Greychurch, her face flushing as red as a beacon.

Red Pete shrugged. 'Gold 'n' silver belong to them who take it.'

'I won't stand for that kind of talk, I'm in charge of the *Pirate Watch*!' she said firmly.

'You may pirate watch if ye wish, dear lady. Raise a flag if ye spot me fair ship. I 'ave to find me cabin boy, Tom, and then we're back to sea again, whatever the mermaid plans.'

'Your cabin boy? ' Mrs Greychurch threw up her hands in horror, shoved the pirate out of her way and rushed along the path yelling, 'Mirandaaaa! Come back!'

'I'm guessin' Tom's alive, then. Thought as much,' chuckled Red Pete, struggling to his feet. 'So why's he hidin' out here on the Isle?' He looked out to sea, where in the distance he thought he saw the mermaid's tail. 'What've ye said to young Tom Lucke, sea witch?' He put his hand to his side where the sword should rest and frowned. 'An' what 'ave ye done with me fine silver sword?' A pirate captain without a sword or a ship was no threat to anyone.

CHAPTER THIRTEEN

TO CHESIL BEACH

While Penfold Lucke stopped off at the Easton pet shop to buy cat food and chat about Groover, Isabel slipped away. She wandered across the Isle, hoping to find some sign of the cabin boy. The sky was deep blue softening to rosy pink at the horizon. Isabel walked past the St George's Centre and then along the narrow cliff path, heading towards Chesil. She watched the sea cool from blue to silver as the sun sank low in the sky. A soft breeze shuddered through the sprigs of scurvy grass that grew along the path, and sent ripples in delicate patterns over the sea.

A black-backed gull soared over her and Isabel watched its flight into the skies over Chesil, where clouds shaped into a silver ship with billowing sails and gun ports. She blinked as the clouds slowly drifted away. On the sea, a ship rocked gently in the waves that rolled towards the pebble arc of Chesil Beach. The ship's honey-coloured wood gleamed in the golden light of the setting sun.

'The *Fortune*!' exclaimed Isabel. She ran along the steep winding track and past the beach huts that dotted the slopes leading down to Chesil Beach.

'I should've fathomed this afore now.' Flintlock stepped out in front of her, barring her way, his arms folded across his chest and black hat pulled low over his eyes. 'I knew some witchery was afoot. That ship appears and disappears like a ghost at yer will.' He grasped Isabel by the arm and pulled her along. 'Come wi' me. I'll not board a ghost ship alone.'

'Let go,' shouted Isabel, swinging a kick at his shins.

'Ouch! What enchantment's this? Bringing ships out o' the sea!

I've searched many a day for the *Fortune*, then it appears with no more 'n a blink o' your eye.' Flintlock looked at the village of Chiswell, the colourful cottages dotted along streets that wound up the steep hillside. 'Hardly know this place. Even the wells are gone. The ole fishmonger, the fine stables, the wash-house, the blacksmith with his forge. Vanished.'

Flintlock dragged Isabel along the stretch of pebbled beach to a fisherman's boat on Chesil bank. 'Let us find Red Pete and see what he has to say 'bout this weird magic.' He pulled the rowing boat down the steeply sloping beach to the water.

'I have to speak to Red Pete too.' Isabel climbed into the boat, holding on to the sides as it tipped in the waves rolling on to Chesil.

Flintlock glared at Isabel, gripping the oars and rowing against the swell towards the silent ship. 'Why?' he demanded.

'I think someone's going to take the *Fortune*,' said Isabel. Eddies in the water swirled around them, catching the oars and twirling the small boat.

'Keep out of 'is business. Interfering witches like thee get dunked in Weston pond,' snarled Flintlock.

'There isn't a pond in Weston any more, and you won't find blacksmiths in Chiswell either. You're a time traveller. It's all different now!' said Isabel. A white kittiwake swooped over them and circled the highest mast of the ship.

Flintlock sat back and flipped the oars out of the water. 'A time traveller, indeed,' he remarked. Caught in the tide, the boat floated towards the hull of the ship. 'Mostly I think this is a dream, young witch, and I'll waken any moment. As for time, 'tis like the sea. A man can sail any way he pleases 'cross time. Once I've found Red Pete and sorted matters with him, I'll find me way home.'

Dipping one oar into the sea, he turned the boat around until they bumped alongside the *Fortune*. The small rowing boat bobbed in the waves like a minnow beside a whale. Waves hushed around the bow and the ship creaked in the water. Rows of gun ports were set in the golden, curved sides of the ship. Three tall masts reached into the sky.

Flintlock held the oars above the waves, water dripping gently. 'Don't like the look o' this. Red Pete was never so quiet. Where is he? And his crew?'

A rope hung from the ship and, finding footholds in the gun ports, he climbed up to the deck. Isabel grasped the rough hemp rope and scaled the steep side of the ship after him. She followed Flintlock's hand- and footholds, as if she were climbing a cliff with Alfie and Peggy. Beneath her hands, the ship felt icy cold. Her breath left puffs of mist in the air. The sky darkened quickly to a deep indigo as the sun dipped below the horizon. Isabel shivered. Drops of water fell from the rigging with a slow drip, drip.

She trailed Flintlock from the main deck into a cabin, crowded with crates of vegetables, bags of flour, biscuits, caskets of water and barrels of salted meat. 'Enough food here for a voyage to France or beyond,' Flintlock noted, rummaging in a box. 'I'll check the quarter deck.'

Isabel listened to the eerie quiet of the ship after he left. She tiptoed to the next cabin, almost expecting to see berths with sleeping pirates. But the small space was stacked with more crates and chests. She heard footsteps overhead and Flintlock appeared from the deck.

'No one aboard,' he declared. 'Why would they leave? The cannon and powder are valuable. Even their matchlocks lie here, abandoned.' He pointed out a heap of guns left in a wooden crate.

The ship swayed gently in the waves. Isabel remembered her dream of the *Fortune* sailing under the beams of the lighthouse and vast waves crashing over the ship. She left the cabins, scrambling past crates and barrels, suddenly desperate to be on deck where she could see the tranquil sea. She looked towards the shore, where the setting sun reflected gold and red in the windows of Chiswell houses. She climbed over rope stays that secured the masts and stood by the ship's wheel. Here, Red Pete had taken the helm during the storm, bringing the *Fortune* back to Portland. She walked to the bow, where she and the cabin boy had clung to the mermaid figurehead.

Flintlock followed her, looking around warily. He nodded at the cold mermaid. 'She's the spirit of the ship, a siren. Many years ago, a mermaid sang to Red Pete, calling him to the sea. I told him 'e dreamt of her, nothing more. Yet her songs changed him. He talked of nothin' but the sea and its hidden treasures. Yet before he fell into her hands, he fled the Isle. They say the mermaid waits for him to return.'

Isabel touched the mermaid's icy turquoise and gold tail.

'Perhaps the Siren's lured all the pirates to a watery grave,' whispered Flintlock. He pointed across the sweep of waves along Chesil Beach. 'A sea monster lurks here too, a fiendish creature that rises from Chesil waves. Some folk see a great fish with a curved tail, others a giant sea horse. The fishermen call it Veasta, a dragon of the sea. They won't fish here when the moon's as thin as a knife over a still sea.'

The ship shuddered in eddies of small waves as the wind whistled through the rigging. The pebbles of Chesil Beach curved along the Fleet into the mists of Moonfleet. 'Let's leave this godforsaken ship,' shivered Flintlock.

Glad to abandon the spookily deserted *Fortune*, Isabel climbed down the rope and jumped into the small boat. Flintlock followed her and rowed them steadily towards the shore into a warmer breeze, the great waves of Chesil rolling them towards the pebbled beach. Isabel trailed her fingers in the sea. In the depths, she imagined green mermaid eyes watching her, waiting and scheming. Isabel snatched her hand out of the water. A copper-coloured moon hung over the island, bathing the sea in strips of gold. As suddenly as it had appeared, the *Fortune* vanished again.

CHAPTER FOURTEEN

SEEKING THE LOST PIRATES

The following morning, Mrs Greychurch hummed as she polished a silver candlestick in the dining room of Groves Farm. She worked her way around the room, dusting and tidying. She liked to pop in to clean the farmhouse from time to time as Mrs Groves neglected the housework, preferring to spend time with the horses and Gregor. Today she had gone to Dorchester, taking a heavy bag with her.

Mrs Greychurch peered at the old paintings around the room. Here was Joseph Groves, painted in 1616, a fine swaggering man. Then kindly Robert Groves and fiery haired Stella with her horse. Suzie pottered around beside her with a fluffy feather duster, wearing Mrs Groves' old green dressing gown which was dragging in a trail behind her. Every now and then she poked Gregor, who was shaking a pink slipper snaffled from the shoe cupboard. He growled and rolled around, ripping into it.

'Good boy,' said Mrs Greychurch, distracted. 'Miranda, tidy things over the fireplace so I can dust.'

Sulkily, Miranda shoved some ornaments into a heap. She sneezed. 'It's dusty in here. I want to go to Chesil skate park today. And these cats are in my way,' she added, glaring at two baskets lined up against the wall, holding the cats. Nellie miaowed at Miranda.

'She doesn't like you,' growled Suzie.

'I don't like your smelly cats either,' snapped Miranda, aiming a kick at the basket.

'Now, now,' said Mrs Greychurch. 'You girls should be grateful that I'm taking you out today. After all, a lot of youngsters have nothing to do in the summer holidays. And here we are, having a lovely time together.' Suzie whacked Miranda across the back of her heels with her duster.

'Yeow! That stings,' squealed Miranda.

Just then, a shadow fell across the floor. 'Who are you?' announced Flintlock from the doorway, removing his hat and staring at Mrs Greychurch. His light brown hair lay flat across his head.

'Ah, you must be Mr Groves. So nice to meet you,' Mrs Greychurch smiled silkily at Flintlock, showing rows of shining teeth against her bright orange lipstick.

'This is my mother,' explained Miranda, 'and that's Suzie.'

'Ah, another household angel. Nice to see ye all doing some work.'

Gregor spat out the slipper and went over to Flintlock, leaning against his legs and gazing up at him with round eyes. Flintlock scratched Gregor's head.

Suzie hauled Surfer out of his basket. 'It's time for Surfer to wake up now. He's a snoozy cat,' she explained, draping him, still asleep, over her shoulder.

Miranda sneezed. 'Aachoo! I'm allergic to that cat. I have to go and look for Tom today.'

'If you mean that awful boy with a long coppery fringe, you can forget it,' snapped Mrs Greychurch. 'I don't approve of fringes, or pirates,' she added, sweeping a duster across the mantelpiece.

Flintlock leaned against the doorway, looking thoughtful. 'Tom Lucke. Why's he lurkin' on the island?'

'He's *my* friend,' sniffed Miranda, wiping her nose on a soggy tissue.

'Is he now?' said Flintlock. 'Well, mind how you deal with him. You missed a bit over there. It's still dusty. Do you know where to find the other pirates?'

'Not yet, but I'm in charge of *Pirate Watch*,' said Mrs Greychurch bossily. 'Those pirates think they can ride rough-shod over us Portlanders, but I plan to vanquish the pirate menace. I'm going to use my cannon to blow their ship to smithereens.'

Flintlock raised his eyebrows. 'Take care not to miss, then. Red

Pete has enough cannon on the *Fortune* to blow Portland sky high, if he pleases.'

Isabel walked along the road through Wakeham into a cool morning mist. Cutting below Pennsylvania Castle, she took the path towards the ruin of St Andrew's Church, past the tree where the owl slept. She stopped, thinking she could hear footsteps behind her. There was a rustle of leaves, the snap of a twig. She climbed into the low branches of a nearby oak, finding footholds in the gnarled trunk.

A gentle breeze hushed through the oak tree. The leaves shook and a small hand pushed aside an acorn. A fairy tumbled and rolled to a halt on the branch beside her. She stood up and shook out her gauzy wings.

'Rainbow!' cried Isabel, greeting the Southwell fairy. She had helped Isabel search for the phantom Black Dog a few months before. Wearing a tricorn hat and breeches, the fairy perched on the branch. She rested her chin in her hands, crossed her legs and looked at Isabel with slanting blue eyes under dark eyebrows.

'What are you doing up a tree?' asked Rainbow in a small, high voice.

'Hiding. I like your hat.'

'Pirates are the latest thing on Portland,' said Rainbow.

'So it would seem,' said Isabel, admiring the fairy's pirate outfit. 'Have you met Captain Red Pete?'

'I've seen him wandering the Isle,' said the fairy, tying the tiny lace on her skull and crossbones boot. 'I remember him from a long time ago. He used to sit by the shore, listening to the mermaid sing.'

'I'm trying to work out how to send him back to the past, where he belongs,' said Isabel.

The fairy looked sideways at Isabel. 'His cabin boy too?' A twig snapped nearby, as if someone trod lightly through the trees.

'Everyone's heard of Cap'n Tom Lucke, the last Portland pirate,' whispered Rainbow, as she slipped away through the crinkled oak leaves.

'Playin' with the owls?' called Red Pete, shaking the lower branches. He gripped a sturdy branch and climbed up below Isabel, grabbed her foot and tugged. Isabel slid from the branch, twigs snapping around her, and fell from the tree, landing in a pile of dry leaves. Red Pete picked her up by the collar. 'Let's take a walk through the ruins, Miss Maydew, an' talk of ole times. This church 'ere weren't built right. The quarrymen always said so. Built in a fair rush, the church never held the ground proper. No wonder 'tis all fallen. My cousin sang in the choir every Matins, lovely voice, clear as a bell.'

Red Pete pushed Isabel under the small archway into the church ruins as he talked. He removed his hat. His hand gripping her shoulder, he glared at Isabel. 'So come on then. Where's the *Fortune*, Miss Maydew? Have ye magic'd me ship away? Are ye a witch, like the Siren says? Or is that another o' her lies?' He shoved Isabel on to the low stone wall overlooking the sea, where gulls circled the empty bay, and stood in front of her, his arms folded, watching her carefully.

'I haven't done anything to the *Fortune*. I saw your ship near Chesil Beach but it disappeared again.' Isabel fidgeted, uncomfortable under his gaze.

'And me crew?'

Isabel shook her head. Red Pete looked out at the dwindling sea mists. 'I'm wary o' this place. The Isle harbours mermaids an' weird creatures, an' a magic far older than you 'n' me. Witches too, o' course, who spin strange enchantments at their whim.'

'Then why did you return to Portland?' demanded Isabel.

'That storm left our sails in tatters. Repairs had to be made. I had to lighten our load; me vessel was sailin' too low in the sea.' He grabbed Isabel by the shoulders and shook her. 'Cast one o' yer Maydew spells an' bring back my ship!'

Isabel struggled. 'I don't know how to cast spells.'

Red Pete released his grip. 'I 'spect that's the truth, though the mermaid would 'ave me believe otherwise.' He turned to leave.

Isabel caught the sleeve of his coat. 'Wait, I think the mermaid brought you here for a reason.'

'No doubt,' sighed the pirate. 'I used to hear a fair mermaid singin' to me from the sea, songs o' gold, spices an' winds of southern seas. Day after day, she sang of Phoenician ships an' Viking warriors. I fought the enchantment o' the sea. Even me ole friend Flintlock Groves called me a fool. For I was a poor boy. No shoes on me feet. Who was I, to hear a mermaid sing? I feared her call so I ran away to seek my fortune, leavin' the Isle and the Siren's songs behind. Now look at me. A pirate. Trapped without a ship, crew or even a sword.'

Red Pete raised his hand in farewell to Isabel, turning to walk deeper into the woods with a swirl of his long black coat. Isabel saw that his curved silver sword had indeed gone. In the speckled sunlight under a sycamore tree he hesitated. Thin beams of sunlight danced over him, sparkling like gold coins on his black coat.

'Find my cabin boy, Miss Maydew. Help 'im if you can,' he called. Isabel blinked. Red Pete had vanished into the green and gold shade of the summer trees.

CHAPTER FIFTEEN

JOLLY ROGER

'Come on, everyone!' bellowed Mrs Greychurch, stamping across a meadow scattered with buttercups by the lighthouse at Portland Bill. 'I've made lunch for us all. We had so much fun earlier, cleaning the farmhouse. Shame you missed it, Isabel.'

Miranda, Suzie and Isabel followed her, lugging a picnic basket, with Penfold Lucke carrying a packet of biscuits. He stayed close to Isabel, like a shark tracking a seal. Gregor ran in circles, sniffing the ground. He started to dig furiously. Mrs Greychurch swatted his tail with a cushion. 'Naughty dog.' Gregor sat down with a thump and glared at her.

Mrs Greychurch found a flat area surrounded by thistles and threw down a checked rug.

'She made me leave my cats at the farm,' Suzie complained to Isabel, tugging at her sleeve.

'They're tired,' said Mrs Greychurch, unpacking bananas and squashed fairy cakes from the basket and placing them on the rug. Gregor darted behind her, snaffling the cakes.

'After lunch, I want us all to look for the pirate ship. A Jolly Roger is flying out there, bringing terror to local shipping.'

'Yes, I'm sure Isabel knows where the *Fortune*'s anchored,' said Penfold. 'She can lead the way.'

'Is that so?' asked Mrs Greychurch, poised above the picnic hamper with a tomato in her hand.

'Isabel doesn't know anything,' said Miranda, sneakily kicking Isabel's ankle. Isabel stared at her coldly.

Suzie adjusted her pirate hat and snatched a fishing net from the basket. 'I'm gonna catch some fish for my cats' tea.'

'Don't wander far,' reminded Isabel. Suzie nodded and ran towards the shore with her fishing rod, Gregor close behind her. Miranda tipped some orange juice into a cup and slurped it.

'I'm going to Chiswell later,' said Penfold, relaxing on the rug. 'I want to explore the beach to do some research for my book. The huge waves have wrecked several pirate ships on Chesil Bank; *Zenobia*, *Lady Isobel*. You can come with me, Isabel. We can visit Pirate's Cove by the Fleet too.'

Miranda screwed up her eyes. 'I think there's a mermaid in the sea.'

'Don't be ridiculous,' sniffed Mrs Greychurch.

'Um, I'm going to check on Suzie,' said Isabel. Penfold scrambled to his feet to follow her.

'Mr Lucke, please count the fairy cakes again. I brought 25 and we only seem to have four, and they're all slobbery,' fussed Mrs Greychurch.

Glad to escape from Penfold, Isabel ran to the shore. Layers of rock formed steps to the sea, their surface marked by the waves of long ago. A mist was creeping along the coast, like an armada of ghost ships.

'Wraaff!' Gregor greeted Isabel with a rock. He dropped it on her toe. She threw the stone back into the sea and Gregor watched the splash. He whined.

'What's the matter, Gregor?' He shook out his fur.

'OK, let's find Suzie. She's wandered off again.' They walked along the rocky shore towards the teetering pile of Pulpit Rock. Suzie was perched on a jutting rock nearby, her feet dangling in the sea spray. The mermaid lurked beside her, flicking her red hair, her tail twined around the rock.

'Suzie!' shouted Isabel. The mermaid rested her hand lightly on Suzie's arm and smiled coldly.

'Wraaff!' Gregor jumped into the sea with a splash and paddled towards the rock.

Suzie was chatting to the mermaid. 'So then I rescued Nellie.

She was wandering around for days and was very hungry. I've had Surfer quite a while, I can't home him 'cos he's always asleep. I've homed Groover though.'

Gregor paddled around them in a circle. The mermaid hissed at him and curled her tail out of the water. She called to Isabel, 'Suzie and I are great friends now. Perhapss I should take her with me.'

Isabel scrambled across the boulders and teetered on the edge of a narrow zigzag of rock. 'Leave her alone!' she shouted.

'We can share the ssecrets of old island magic and look for the giant who sleepss,' taunted the mermaid.

'So there really *is* an island giant?' asked Suzie.

'Of course,' said the mermaid.

Gregor scrambled on to the rock behind Suzie. He shook a spray of salt water over the mermaid who, with a last glance at Isabel, slithered into the sea, disappearing beneath the water. Gregor nudged Suzie with his nose. 'Hello, Blackbeard, the pirate dog.' She patted him, scrambled to her feet and balanced along the edge of the jutting rocks towards Isabel, with Gregor following close behind her, shaking the water from his fur.

'Hello,' called Ben cheerily, crunching along the path from the car park. 'I drove down with Peggy in the *Jolly Roger* van. It rattles like crazy. I took some photos on my iPhone. Have a look. That's me in front of the van. Here's where we're driving along, and that's my arm. It got in the way.'

'Great!' said Isabel.

'Caught any fish today, Suzie?' Ben asked.

Suzie was wading across a small rock pool, clutching her fishing net. 'Nah, I've been talking to a mermaid.' Gregor pounced on her and snatched the net between his teeth, dashing up to Ben with his prize.

'Of course, there *are* bottlenose dolphins around the shores of Portland,' said Ben.

'She's got sharp teeth,' Suzie remarked.

'And basking sharks,' he added. 'Anyway, I just came to remind you that you're going climbing today. Remember?'

'I'd forgotten,' admitted Isabel.

'You're going to drop Gregor off at the farm on the way,' added Ben. He clipped on Gregor's lead and tried to tug the fishing net from the dog's teeth. Delighted, Gregor edged backwards, pulling Ben with him. 'I'm not playing, Gregor. Let go!'

'Harrumph!' said Gregor, releasing the net. Ben fell sideways into the pool.

Suzie looked thoughtful. 'I'd like to rescue that mermaid. She's nice. I could keep 'er at home.'

Isabel shook her head. 'I don't think she wants to be rescued.'

'I think she likes *me* a lot more than you,' said Suzie, looking out to sea.

Pirates Bill and Shorty attached hammocks to the apple trees behind Lucke Cottage and sank comfortably into their new quarters, with the budgie hopping from branch to branch between them, fluffing out his yellow cheeks and whistling. A Jolly Roger flag caught the breeze at the top of a tree.

'Nip into the kitchen for ham 'n' biscuits, Gunner Hardy,' ordered Mr Otter, reclining on a deck chair with one of Penfold's flowery shirts over his own tattered clothes. 'Has our good sailmaker Bleet blowed up that fish raft? It may come in useful if we can find us an oar.'

Bleet was puffing into an inflatable whale. Hardy jumped over the whale and climbed through the window of the cottage to collect food.

''Tis a good likeness to nature, that fish,' chortled Bill. 'Mr Otter'll 'ave one o' them cooked up for our tea!'

Mr Otter, Ship's Cook, patted his round stomach. He thrust a dagger into a tin of beans, scooping off the lid, and wolfed them with his fingers. 'Fine victuals, no need fer fish,' he blurted, a stack of ten tins laid out beside him. 'I'm takin' this lot aboard wi' me. Summat fer later when we're at sea agin. Pass me yer handkercher.'

'What about Tom?' asked Bill. 'Red Pete 'ad fine plans fer 'im. Work 'im hard, show 'im the ropes.'

Hardy returned with a packet of Rich Tea biscuits. He shook his head. 'Cutlass 'as been whisperin' in Tom's ear for weeks.'

Mr Otter nodded. 'I tol' Red Pete. Cutlass has his eye on Spanish treasure. He can't eat nor sleep for thinkin' about the finery o' that gold 'n' silver.'

'The gold's mine,' squawked the budgie.

'Aye,' agreed Mr Otter. 'Whassat noise?'

The pirates listened to footsteps approaching along the garden path. Alfie appeared around the corner of Lucke Cottage, with loops of climbing rope over his shoulder.

'Why, 'tis young Alfie!' cried Shorty, jumping from the hammock. 'Haven't seen 'im in ages! Look ee, all growed up. 'Tis the lad who waved from Southwell! Remember how ee rowed his little boat out to us an' climbed aboard to see the cannon?'

'I remember it well, though it's been 9 years since,' said Alfie, shaking Shorty's hand.

'Niver!' cried Shorty, 'jus' a matter o' months. This is a darklin' place. 'Tis no wonder Red Pete steers clear o' the Isle an' the wicked sea nymph. Yet here we are! Stranded like a bunch o' frogs by a dry puddle.'

'Where's Captain Red Pete?' asked Alfie.

Shorty shook his head sadly. 'We're in a terrible fix 'ere, young friend. Red Pete's lost, his cabin boy Tom's gorn a'wanderin'. As fer Cutlass, he's gone mad for gold, an' Flintlock Groves is gallopin' about on our tails. We're hidin' here till we find the ship again.'

''Ave a tin o' fine fodder, young Alfie. I say Red Pete's a fool fer not tellin' Tom who ee really is. I don't hold with secrets. Sit yerself down,' said Mr Otter, pointing at the whale.

Alfie perched nervously on the whale, which deflated with a slow oommmph. 'Ah muzzens, ye'll 'ave to puff 'im up again, Bleet. Pass me a slice o' porker, Alfie,' added Mr Otter.

'I have to go. I'm climbing the West Cliffs later,' said Alfie, struggling to his feet.

'Aye, we have to find our ship and leave soon, if t'isn't hidden in the depths o' the ocean by the sea witch,' said Shorty.

The other pirates nodded in agreement.

Mrs Groves tiptoed into the dark stable with Gregor, still damp from his swim in the sea. As she had guessed, the boy was sleeping curled up in the corner on bales of straw, wrapped in Isaac's woollen blanket. She peered down at him. His face was smudged with dirt and he was sound asleep. Next to him on the straw was a long curved sword.

Mrs Groves sat down on a bale with a plate of cheese and biscuits on her lap to wait until the boy woke up. Gregor snuffled around the stable, digging under drifts of loose straw. 'Stop it,' she whispered. Gregor shook out his fur and jumped up at Mrs Groves. She patted him, then pushed him away. 'You smell fishy, Gregor.' He padded to the boy, sniffed him and licked his face. Tom woke up with a start.

'Don't be alarmed,' said Mrs Groves quickly. 'I've been leaving food out for you at the farmhouse.'

The boy sat up slowly. 'I'll pay for the food, Missus.'

'No need,' said Mrs Groves kindly. 'Please stop licking his face, Gregor.' Gregor leaped onto the straw bale and draped himself across the boy's lap, panting hot breath over him. 'Who are you?' she asked.

'My name's Tom Lucke.'

'Ah yes, I've heard of you,' she said, sizing up the boy as a visitor from another time, like Flintlock. She remembered reading about an infamous pirate captain of that very name, born on Portland over 300 years ago. Yet this boy seemed far too young to command a pirate ship. 'Tell me, what brought you here, Tom?'

'A storm and a mermaid,' began Tom. Mrs Groves sat back to listen to his story. He told her about his life as a cabin boy on the *Fortune*, climbing the rigging and capturing ships to plunder their treasure. When he leaped to his feet and showed how Cutlass had taught him to wield a sword, she gasped, 'Good grief!'

Other than this, Mrs Groves listened quietly, until Tom told her about the witch Isabel Maydew. 'Now I can help you with this, as I know Isabel very well,' she interrupted.

Hidden by the stable door, Flintlock leaned with his arms folded, listening to Mrs Groves talking to the cabin boy. From time to time he shook his head. 'I 'ave to find Red Pete as soon as I can, before we're all doomed to stay trapped 'ere forever,' he muttered.

CHAPTER SIXTEEN

WALK THE PLANK

'Put your foot there, Isabel,' called Peggy. She pulled the rope at the top of *Walk the Plank* climb near Blacknor. Isabel adjusted the strap of her blue safety helmet and moved her foot to another small nook in the cliff. Alfie climbed just ahead of her, attached to Isabel's harness with another length of rope.

A rope also looped further down the cliff to Ryder. 'Right behind you, Izzie,' he shouted. 'Which part of the cliff do I climb next, Alfredo?'

'Swing your arm up, Ryder,' said Alfie.

Isabel slowly made her way up the cliff. She found a firm handhold and lifted her foot up to a narrow crevice. From there, she levered herself on to a ledge. A stone shifted, bounced down the cliff face and pinged off a rock.

Alfie paused just above Isabel, attaching a Quickdraw clip to a bolt secured in the rock, and leaned back in his harness.

Her fingers and arms aching, Isabel looked across the glistening blue water of Lyme Bay. She saw a small fin in the water. 'A sunfish!' she cried excitedly.

'Could be,' Alfie replied. 'Climbers often see amazing things from up here. I've watched smugglers walking up the path from Blacknor Rock.' He pointed towards a dark smooth rock, tilted just above the sea. 'A young woman with a long plait in her hair stood there one day and spoke to a beautiful mermaid. And a boy ran by the rock pools with a spear in his hand and a pack of wolves at his heels. I even saw a great sea dragon, flying so close I could have touched his green and gold scales. Out here on the cliffs, time doesn't mean anything at all, Izzie.'

'You never told me this before!' exclaimed Isabel.

Alfie shrugged. 'I prefer to keep things to myself. People don't always believe in mermaids and dragons.'

'Peggy says you grew up in the village of Southwell,' said Isabel.

'That's right. I lived in Old Smithy cottage, overlooking the sea to the south of Portland.'

'Did you ever see a ship called the *Fortune*?' she asked.

Alfie hesitated, and then nodded. 'Why d'you ask?' He attached his clip to another metal loop in the rock-face, his eyes turned away from Isabel.

'The *Fortune* returned to Portland, but the ship has disappeared, and the pirates are stranded here,' she said. 'Captain Red Pete's wandering the Isle, and his cabin boy Tom's lost too. As for the crew, I haven't even seen them.'

Alfie adjusted the rope running through the clip. 'My guess is that the ship'll turn up. Red Pete and the pirate crew will have to leave together, though. They can't set sail without their captain.'

'What about their cabin boy?' asked Isabel.

Alfie shrugged. 'Not as important, I guess, as the ship's captain. Let's tackle the last part of the climb now. Ryder's catching up with us.'

A few minutes later, Isabel stood at the top of the cliff helping Alfie organise the ropes, clips and harnesses. He held the rope over his arm, winding it into big loops. Peggy kneeled on the grass, sorting through the Quickdraw clips. Nearby a small cluster of bee orchids grew in the dry soil. Ryder had also reached the top of the cliff and was sitting on the grass with his legs crossed, strumming a ukulele and singing loudly, 'Twas Friday morn when we set sail, and we were not far from the land, when the captain he spied a lovely mermaid, with a comb and a glass in her hand.'

Isabel looked out to sea, wondering about the pirates and watching the gentle swell of the waves. She closed her eyes, feeling the warm sunlight wrap around her like a cloak. She remembered the sea dragon and the friendly snow wolves. A shadow loomed over her. The breeze ruffled her hair and clouds floated across the inside of her eyes, faster and faster. Isabel crouched down and clutched the spiky shoots of grass as time shifted and crumbled around her, falling away like tumbling cliffs. She heard a deep booming roar. Isabel felt as if she were travelling very fast through space, and then suddenly stopped. She flew forwards and landed in the grass. Slowly she opened her eyes, to find herself in a strange, unfamiliar place.

Ryder, Peggy and Alfie had vanished. The grass around her grew tall and golden-yellow flowers bloomed everywhere. Bees hummed from flower to flower.

'It's all different!' she gasped. She scrambled to her feet. Across the fields she saw a row of houses built around a pond that sparkled in the sunlight. She looked towards the now small village of Weston, thinking about the cabin boy, Tom Lucke. She decided that she disagreed with Alfie. The cabin boy *was* important, perhaps more so than anyone else from the *Fortune*. Rescued by the devious mermaid, he was the key to the fate of the *Fortune*. And Isabel had travelled across time to prove this.

At Weston pond, boys idly skimmed stones across the water. A row of houses overlooked them, windows thrown wide open and white sheets catching the breeze on a washing line. Two girls and a boy were playing hopscotch nearby. Isabel looked around the small village, recalling how grey the houses looked in old black and white photographs of Portland, making the past seem a colourless place. Yet the old village of Weston was clustered around a clear blue pond, the houses built from fresh white Portland stone. The grass around the pond grew long and green, dotted with tall cowslips.

She walked around the pond, following a group of women carrying baskets to a crossroads, then past the Tudor house with its small dark windows, surrounded by an elegant garden with fountains and statues. Ahead she recognised the thatched cottages of Gypsy Lane.

Isabel hesitated, unsure which route to take. She turned towards the east coast, scuffing her trainers in the dry mud. To the south lay sloping meadows and the sea beyond sparkled silver and blue. To the north, windmills turned gently in the breeze. Horses grazed on patches of grass by the track and carts leaned against small cottages dotted at the side of the narrow road. Isabel wondered who lived in the sleepy thatched cottages. She saw a scythe resting against a stone wall. Beside another low cottage with latticed windows were a tangle of fishing nets and slatted boxes.

As she walked along the sunlit track, children ran from the backyards and stared at her, jumping over the tumbledown stone walls and shouting to one another, 'Come and look at this lady!' They pointed at her and whispered. Isabel noticed the boys' short breeches and the girls' long skirts. She saw men in felt workmen's hats returning home for lunch from their labour in the fields. A brown and white horse and low cart jostled past her, carrying a weight of Portland stone. The driver flicked a glance at her and reined in the horse.

'Where you headin'?' he called.

'The Lucke Cottage,' replied Isabel. He pointed ahead with a stubby finger and clicked at the horse to continue. Isabel approached the cottage, feeling butterflies in her stomach. The house looked tidier than the present-day home of Penfold Lucke, the steps to the gate scrubbed and the yard swept clean. A woman in a grey bodice and skirt bustled out with two girls. She stood by the doorway in a stone slabbed porch and wiped her hands on her apron, staring at Isabel.

'Ye must be one o' them Maydew children, in those new-fangled clothes,' she stated. 'An' you got the same nose 'n' eyes as prim and proper Lucy Maydew, who teaches school over at Rayfourn. Father's workin' in the fields, if 'tis him ye seek.' The girl folded her arms. 'I'm Beth.' Her eyes were the vivid blue of forget-me-nots, shrewd and kind. In the yard, a mangle waited with a basket of washing.

Pails of water stood around the yard, by baskets of green apples and a pile of potato peelings. A girl was scrubbing the peeled potatoes.

One of the children tugged her sleeve. 'Beth, is she a witch from West Cliff?' A small girl in a deep-blue dress with a frayed hem came from the cottage and looked at Isabel curiously. She giggled and whispered to two boys, who also stared at her. Isabel looked down at her red t-shirt and jeans and realised how strange she must seem to the children.

'Take care o' the washing,' said Beth to the girl. 'The rest of ye can run along whilst I talk to our visitor and see what she wants o' us.'

By the porch, the boys crouched down to work on a small model of a ship. One of them looked up. 'Is Tom comin' back?'

Beth threw open the rickety gate, closed it carefully behind her and approached Isabel. Her dark red hair was pulled back tightly in a bun, pinned neatly at the nape of her neck.

'I know Tom Lucke,' said Isabel.

'You're the same age, I guess. Those boys are Tom's cousins. He lived wi' us. His only brother went to sea many years ago. What brings you from over yonder?' She nodded her head towards the west.

'I'm heading for the coast, to find a ship called the *Fortune*.'

'That's a dangerous ship to seek, pirates an' all,' said Beth. She put her hand to her throat where a gold cross set with three diamonds glinted in the sun. It seemed at odds with her simple grey bodice, a thin line of lace at the collar and two buttons on the narrow sleeves. 'If ye find the *Fortune*, tell Peter ...' the woman tailed off, as a movement in the apple trees beside the yard caught her eye. She glanced over her shoulder quickly and raised her voice. 'We don't talk to strangers, young miss. Be on your way.' She caught Isabel quickly by the hand. 'Tell him to take care o' Tom. I worry for him,' she whispered.

Isabel felt the girl's eyes on her as she walked away from the cottage through a small orchard of apple and pear trees. At the end of the track, the route forked. Curious, Isabel ventured further into the village of Wakeham, noticing how wide and smooth the road seemed compared to the track from Weston. She found a low dark barn, and then a row of tidy cottages set back from the street. Children ran down the hill towards her with a large wooden hoop, spinning it with a stick and roaring with laughter. A small girl clutching a rag doll stopped and stared at her. Isabel waved and the girl smiled back. She turned towards the house she knew as the Portland Museum, looking curiously at the small cottage, with its stone walls and golden thatched roof.

Isabel turned south, heading away from Wakeham. Climbing over a wall, she followed a footpath lined with bramble bushes into a pasture where Portland sheep grazed peacefully. In the distance, cows wandered on a narrow strip of land. It was quieter here, away from the busy villages of Weston and Wakeham, the only sound the thin song of a skylark. Isabel looked up at the tiny speck high in the blue sky, below a white drifting cloud. Slowly the cloud took shape, forming sails and masts.

Someone wrenched her arm behind her back. 'What d'you want 'ere, Miss?'

'Ow!' yelled Isabel. She swung her heel back sharply.

Cutlass released her and bent double. 'That's me knee, you fiend. I've no end o' trouble with it. The damp on board ship ruins 'em.'

Isabel glared at him. 'You startled me.'

Cutlass rubbed his leg, scowling. 'What d'ye want at Lucke Cottage?'

'Why does it concern you?' she demanded, glowering at the pirate.

'Yer a fine madam, aren't ye?' gasped Cutlass. 'I seen ye snoopin' an' askin' all manner o' questions. What are ye lookin' for?'

'Same as you, I expect. I'm looking for a ship called the *Fortune*,' said Isabel. Cutlass limped towards her and she stepped out of his way. But the pirate was looking out to sea, his eyes wide with amazement. Anchored by Cheyne Weares, the *Fortune* had reappeared.

'Just as ye spake, there she is!' he said, unsheathing a dagger from his belt. 'No more o' yer witchery. Come along nicely an' join me aboard.' He grasped her arm and pushed her towards the ship. Beyond the brambles, he turned onto a narrow path that twisted through the rocks, down steps to a small boat on the shore. 'That's our boat, clinker built with overlapping pieces o' wood. Tarred to keep out the sea. A young lad, Tom Lucke, sawed all them strips o' wood. Built it with me. I've a fondness for that lad, I s'pose. If ee wasn't a Lucke, I'd like 'im more,' grumbled Cutlass.

Minutes after Cutlass and Isabel had rowed out and climbed aboard the *Fortune*, the rest of the pirates scrambled down the path after them. 'Ahoy Cutlass!' called Shorty, waving the Jolly Roger flag. He was carrying a blown-up whale under his other arm. 'I see the *Fortune*'s back at last! Bleet saw a cloud shaped like a ship wi' masts an' sails all ragged from a storm. T'was a sign. Ee led the way here.' Shorty patted Bleet on the back. 'Well done, lad.'

The other pirates clattered after them. Mr Otter was lugging a large supermarket bag full of tins. Bleet and Hardy were transporting a flowery armchair that Isabel was sure she had seen at Lucke Cottage.

'Have ye got the tea-set?' demanded Mr Otter.

Shorty nodded. 'Bill's got it.'

Bill teetered behind them, carrying the tea-set carefully on a tray. ''Tis too dainty. I'm afeared o' droppin' it.' A clock chimed under his arm.

'Hush that thing up, Bill!'

Isabel turned to Cutlass. 'Have they been staying at Lucke Cottage?'

Cutlass poked her. 'Never ye mind where they been. Wait 'ere while I row back to fetch 'em.' The *Fortune* rocked as waves lapped against her gleaming golden bow. Cutlass swung down a rope and rowed ashore. The pirates clambered aboard the small rowing boat. Shorty wedged the whale beside him and Bill clutched the tea-set on his knees.

As they reached the *Fortune*, with Cutlass tugging at the oars to pull the heavy boat through the water, Hardy held up his hand to check wind direction. 'Wind's changin' again. We should set sail tonight, Cutlass. Best to make headway by the Shambles sandbanks afore dark.'

Shorty climbed aboard the *Fortune*, flinging the inflated whale ahead of him over the side of the ship. The rest of the pirates followed. Bill hauled himself up a rope with one hand and balanced the tea-set on his shoulder with the other.

'Who's this?' demanded Hardy, staring at Isabel. 'Red Pete don't like strangers aboard.'

'This one's been interferin' at Lucke Cottage,' said Cutlass.

'Throw 'er in the galley. She can make tea in them fancy cups,' called Bill, threading a large needle. 'I'm goin' to start mending the sails.'

Cutlass snarled, 'I reckon she's seekin' our treasure. P'raps she's enchanted Red Pete an' tooken our gold. She's left 'im hoppin' round th' Isle thinkin' ee's some kind o' toad.' He shoved Isabel roughly.

The pirates turned and looked hard at the strange girl.

Mr Otter shrugged, 'Red Pete may be a toad but ee's left us treasure enough, an' barrels o' food and beer.'

Cutlass shook his head angrily. 'With *all* the treasure, we could forgo piratin' an' live in a manor house o' good Portland stone, with glass windows, brushed floors an' kindly maids to fetch 'n' carry. Even the Court Leet what governs th' Isle'll do as we wish, 'cos we'll be fine genteelmen. We can live easy as a churchman if we 'ave all the gold 'n' silver. This girl knows more 'n she tells.' Cutlass jabbed Isabel with his finger.

The clock chimed again.

'Nah, let the girl go, she's a scrap of a thing, no meat on 'er,' said Mr Otter, shaking the clock. 'I like livin' on a ship. 'Tis fine when the wind fills the sails and there's no land in sight, just sea an' sky an' a shoal of tasty fish swimmin' alongside.'

The rest of the crew nodded in agreement.

Cutlass shoved Isabel again and she landed in a pile of hemp rope coiled on the deck. She untangled herself and sat up. 'You can't leave without Red Pete and Tom. You're trapped here until they both return to the ship.'

'Is she bewitchin' us?' demanded Cutlass.

Bill poked her with an oar. 'Nay, she's just a lass.' He held out his hand and pulled Isabel to her feet. 'We ain't leavin' without our Cap'n.'

The other pirates watched her warily as Isabel gazed across the sea, where small waves scudded from the east. A mist was surging like a fleet of ghostly longboats across the water, hiding the low line of cliffs that marked the villages of Osmington and Ringstead. She shuddered.

Hardy followed her gaze. 'We 'ave to find Red Pete. See how the tides and wind are changin', swingin' us to and fro. That anchor at the stern's only just holdin' the ship g'inst the current. Red Pete'll hear if we fire a cannon nigh Church Ope,' he said.

Shorty scratched his forehead and sat on the whale. 'He told us to wait hereabouts for 'im.'

'Ee's been lost ashore for days,' said Bleet.

'You have to find Tom too,' reminded Isabel.

'Don't mind what she says. She's clever, sharp as a blade. I say she's schemin' wi' that Flintlock Groves. I seen 'im ridin' around the Isle like ee's Lord o' the Royal Manor,' said Cutlass.

Shorty shook his head. 'With this nor'easterly wind, we'll 'ave to tack upwind an' sail along the coast.'

'I'll help you look for Red Pete,' insisted Isabel, although she wondered how they would find a pirate who may still be hundreds of years adrift in time. A sea breeze tugged her hair. She looked towards the stretch of shoreline twisting north by Rufus Castle. Clouds were massing along the coast above the small keep.

Bill leaned on a capstan, shaped like a huge cotton-reel drum.

'Red Pete would say we should set sail to find 'im if the crew all agree on it. He's a fair cap'n.'

'The girl's right, we 'ave to find young Tom too,' said Mr Otter, and folded his arms across his stout chest. Some of the crew nodded. 'We 'aven't treated him right. No wonder the boy's hidin' out on the Isle.'

Cutlass scowled. 'Since when did we follow the ship's cook? Tom's better off ashore, I reckon.'

The wind tugged at the ropes on the masts, rattling them like an impatient ghost, and the sea mist poured across the waves towards them. Cutlass looked at the gathering fog and sighed. The crew watched him expectantly. He made a decision. 'All hands on deck! Haul up them anchors!' he shouted. 'Make sail! We'll tack along the coast, find Red Pete an' leave tonight afore the wind runs us on to the rocks.'

Bill and Shorty took the capstan bars to winch the sails, pushing round the huge drums. The sails rose up the masts where they flapped like giant wings, while the pirates secured the ropes.

Cutlass took the helm. 'Bring 'er about fast!' he shouted. 'Make haste! 'Tis time to leave!'

CHAPTER SEVENTEEN

CANNON FIRE

Mrs Groves stood by the oak tree in the field beyond Groves Farm. She looked at her watch and blew her whistle. Ryder took off towards a horse jump with Gregor attached by a rope to Ryder's climbing harness, his baggy shorts billowing. Suzie raced after them.

'Whoopsadaisy,' she yelled as Ryder and Gregor collided with the first jump and fell in a tangled heap. Suzie picked up one of Ryder's enormous flip-flops, which had flown across the field, and Gregor snatched the other.

'We're never going to be ready for the Dog Agility Show at this rate,' Mrs Groves sighed to Ben.

He pulled an earphone from his ear. 'Wha'?'

Flintlock leaned against the oak tree next to Ben, a row of baskets beside him. 'Waste of time. The pair should put in a day's work on the farm. What does Ryder *do* anyway?' he asked, yawning. He stretched out his arms and folded them behind his head. Gregor thundered past him with the flip-flop between his teeth, making a circuit of the field with Ryder chasing him.

'He teaches windsurfing,' said Mrs Groves. Flintlock looked at her blankly.

Ben explained further. 'He has a board with a sail attached and he sails up and down Portland Harbour near the Sailing Academy. Windsurfing's an Olympic sport.'

'Does he fetch an' carry goods from Portland to Sandsfoot Castle over on yonder shore?' asked Flintlock.

'I don't think so,' said Mrs Groves. 'Sometimes he carries his ukulele. My nephew Wolven's a champion windsurfer.'

Ryder made a flying tackle at Gregor and missed, skidding across the grass on his stomach. Gregor chewed into the flip-flop a few feet from him.

Flintlock snorted. 'Tell him he can have a proper job at the farm. We could put 'im and that lazy dog to work in the fields. He can grow wheat an' barley, an' tend to sheep.' Gregor spat out the slobbery flip-flop and rolled wildly on the grass.

'Get up, you bad dog! Your fur will be full of grass seeds!' shrieked Mrs Groves, chasing after Gregor.

Suzie returned from chasing Ryder to inspect her cats. 'Are you keeping an eye on my cats, Mr Groves, like I asked?' she demanded.

'Yes, yes,' said Flintlock, 'though I'm not used to bein' given orders by someone so small.'

Suzie stamped her foot at him. 'It's not my fault I'm only 5 years old!'

In the distance there was an explosion, like cannon fire. The ground shook and a flock of sparrows took off from the Groves oak. For a second, a shadow passed in front of the sun, as if a giant was striding across the island.

'Trouble!' said Flintlock. 'A ship firing out at sea. I reckon that's the *Fortune*.'

'The pirate ship?' asked Mrs Groves.

Flintlock nodded.

Ben closed down his iPhone as Flintlock ran to the stables. He glanced at Suzie, who was looking at him with big, shocked eyes.

'Did you see a giant?' asked Suzie.

'It was a cloud,' said Ben. 'All these paranormal things can be explained. Umm, didn't Isabel mention the *Fortune* the other day?'

Suzie nodded. 'She's lookin' for pirates. I've got a baaaad feeling in my tummy,' she said, rubbing her stomach.

'Would you like a sausage roll?' asked Mrs Groves. 'I made some earlier.' Suzie shook her head.

Ryder galumphed over to them. 'Talking of Izzie, a mysterious thing happened on West Cliff an hour or so ago, after the Izz Meister and I climbed *Walk the Plank* with Alfredo.' He raised his bushy eyebrows and looked from Ben to Suzie.

'What happened?' asked Ben.

'I was singing a song about a mermaid, a fine sea shanty. I'll get my ukulele and play it to you.'

Suzie gripped the edge of his shorts. 'Where's Izzie?' she growled.

'She vanished,' said Ryder. 'Strangest thing I ever saw. One minute she was there, then poof, gone.'

Ben adjusted his hat. 'I think we'd better look for her.'

'I'll come with you,' insisted Ryder. 'Hang on a mo while I change out of my dog training kit.' He whipped off a t-shirt with *Go Gregor* on the front and replaced it with a luminous green shirt that reached almost to his knees. Gregor bounded around him barking frantically. 'Chill out, dog dude,' he said.

'Sit, Blackbeard!' said Suzie. Gregor sat down.

'I'm sure Isabel's fine, but just in case, you can take Gregor with you,' said Mrs Groves. 'He needs a good walk.'

Flintlock was returning from the stables, leading his black horse and carrying a clanking sack. He hugged Mrs Groves. 'Aunt Estelle, this farm's in the best o' hands. Make sure the bills are paid on time and good records kept. I've left you more than enough to have the roof repaired and th' chimneys swept. I've business to finish now with a pirate.'

'Pirates!' Mrs Groves gulped. 'There seem to be a lot of them about at the moment.' She clipped on Gregor's lead and handed it to Ryder.

'Wow,' said Suzie excitedly. She bounced up and down. 'Let's go!'

Flintlock leaped on his horse, turning him with a gentle tug of the reins. He looked thoughtfully towards the east coast. With a final wave to Mrs Groves, he set off at a gentle trot, moving to a gallop as he rode beneath the Groves oak tree, and disappeared from view.

'Kind of a moody dude,' reflected Ryder.

'Isabel's mixed up in this,' said Ben to Suzie. 'We have to find her before she sets sail with a ship full of pirates.'

Isabel clung to a starboard rail as the *Fortune* skimmed over the waves. The wind knotted her hair and made her eyes stream. Beside the ship, a shoal of silver fish darted and twisted. White froth topped the waves as the *Fortune* headed north along the coast of Portland. Rufus Castle stood solidly among sloping meadows.

'Lower the sails!' yelled Cutlass. 'We'll anchor by Church Ope awhile. The young witch can make herself useful an' conjure up Red Pete fer us.'

'I'll get the powder caskets ready. Let's fire another warning shot across th' Isle!' called Shorty.

As the crew anchored the ship, Cutlass pushed Isabel towards the rowing boat, lowering it into the water. Isabel swung down a hemp rope into the boat after Cutlass. He muttered to himself, the boat wobbling from side to side in the waves. Isabel gulped, feeling seasick. Cutlass smirked at her pale face, rowing them slowly ashore, pulling the oars through the darkening water.

A white mist streamed over the cove, swirling like ghosts. Isabel glimpsed a longboat, with a dragon's head and rows of painted shields, sailing stealthily into the still waters of Church Ope. She heard the faint splash of oars as the ghostly longboat vanished. Reaching the shore, Cutlass tugged their boat on to the pearl-grey pebbles of the beach. He hesitated and looked around the small bay. The cove was very still and quiet. Tiny bats rose from the bell tower at St Andrew's Church and flitted into the sky on jagged wings.

Cutlass waved his arms like a windmill. 'Bats! An evil omen! We'll take the run to the north by Rufus Castle. Follow me.' He scuttled towards a path that wound through a windswept meadow up to the castle. Isabel saw her chance to escape. She turned and ran.

'Come back, you varmint!' She heard Cutlass stumbling behind her as she sprinted across the beach to the woods. She zigzagged through the trees and ducked behind a clump of ferns. Cutlass caught up with her and swiped his sword through the bushes as she crawled into a hollow beneath the owl's favourite tree and hid.

Finally, after several minutes, Cutlass gave up the search. Isabel breathed out with relief, uncurling from the roots of the tree. She wanted to find Red Pete herself, without Cutlass interfering. She looked around at the clusters of trees that hid the paths to Wakeham village. Through the branches she saw St Andrew's Church, a low sturdy building tucked into the cliffs.

As she hurried to the church, the ground trembled beneath her feet. Copper and green lights flickered across the sky and Isabel felt time shuddering around her again. A shadow of a giant appeared over the trees for a few seconds, his deep-set eyes like caverns in a cliff face.

'What's happening?' she whispered. Something had changed, but here she was, still in the past. The sun was sinking over the island.

Pushing through brambles, she reached a narrow path leading to the lopsided church set into the cliffs above Church Ope. In the distance she heard the sound of a horse's hooves, drumming the ground. 'Flintlock,' she breathed. She ran along the steep path towards the church. She had to find Red Pete before anyone else.

Ben and Suzie took the winding footpath through the trees towards the bay at Church Ope. Ryder and Gregor skidded behind them with Gregor pulling hard on the leash, wild with excitement.

'Hold on, dog dude, you're going too fast!' yelled Ryder. He veered through the bushes. Ben and Suzie heard him yelling in the distance, 'Stooopp!' There was a scuffle, a lot of barking and eventually a splash.

'There it is! The pirate ship!' yelled Suzie, pointing through the trees. Ben stared, his mouth open. Far below them he saw the shimmering blue seas where a large ship lurked, a skull and crossbones fluttering at the top of its mast.

'Slow down, Suzie,' called Ben, too late, as she tripped head over heels in tangled ivy and rolled like a dormouse into an oak tree. Ahead, the familiar ruins of St Andrew's, with tumble-down walls and overgrown gravestones, had been replaced by a church with a low grey roof and a neat churchyard, the grass cut short around rows of white stones.

'We must be lost,' gasped Ben, helping Suzie to her feet.

'I don't care. I'm goin' on a pirate ship,' yelled Suzie, taking off through the trees again. With a last glance at the church, Ben ran after her.

CHAPTER EIGHTEEN

St Andrew's Church

Isabel stood beneath a tall elm tree, looking at the small church. With a simple stained-glass window overlooking the sea, the low building was surrounded by walls holding it secure to the steep cliff. A slender bell tower stood a few steps from the church. Graves lined the sunlit churchyard. Isabel touched a plain white cross with the name *Mary Atwooll* and lingered by a small stone marked *Abel Flew 1676*. She studied an older cross engraved with leaves, and a square stone with an ornate hourglass. A magpie landed on the low roof of the church, sending loose grey tiles slipping. She walked around the church, looking for Red Pete, hoping he might be here.

Isabel pushed at a creaking door, set into an arch carved with oak leaves and acorns. Letters above the door spelled *Let us go into the house of the Lord.* The old church smelled of wood and leaves, warm like a forest. By the pews, she saw a heap of dark blue books with *Common Prayer Book* on the cover. A thin red and gold rug lay along the aisle. Isabel paused to look at a window showing a saint in a blue robe holding out his hand to a lamb. Isabel tiptoed along the aisle, peering behind stone pillars for Red Pete. The pews and the bases of the pillars were carved with ivy around stone zigzags. By the pulpit she stopped to look at a large Bible, the pages decorated with deep blue paints and gold leaf.

'Evenin'.' Red Pete was sitting in an alcove with his feet up on a pew, leafing through a hymn book and swigging from a bottle of sherry he had plundered from Mrs Greychurch. The budgie was edging along the pew next to him, eyeing Isabel beadily. She sat down in the seat behind him, under the cold gaze of a row of angel statues.

'Red Pete, I've been looking for you,' she whispered.

'Don't bother whisperin'. Just you, me and th' angels in here,' said the pirate.

'Is that your budgie?' asked Isabel.

'I'm his pirate,' said Red Pete wearily. 'Thought I'd lost him to a cat or something.'

'Groover,' agreed the budgie. He tucked his head under his wing to preen his feathers.

Isabel looked around, wonderingly. 'I've never seen a church like this before.'

'Haven't seen St Andrew's meself in a good while,' said Red Pete. He sat back with his arms folded. 'I saw lights in th' heavens an' the ground shook 'neath my feet. Just as if a huge giant strode across the land. Then I found our old church 'ere again.' Red Pete raised his bushy eyebrows at her. 'An' then ye appear too. Some folk may call ye a witch o' great and fearful powers, with time wrapped round 'er little finger.' He looked at Isabel shrewdly. ''Course, I don't say that meself.' He placed the bottle next to him on the pew. 'Yet 'tis a dark mystery, for yesterday, this was a heap o' stone and a few ole graves. Today a church. One day, I'll be buried here meself with a vast block o' stone, an epic poem engraved i' marble, an' a skull 'n' crossbones to scare nosy folk away.'

'People would come from far and wide to see a grave like that,' said Isabel.

'Aye, even from Waymuthe,' agreed Red Pete.

'How old is this building?' asked Isabel.

Red Pete looked around the church. 'Built in 1475, long time ago. The chancel at the front faces east towards the sunrise.' He rose to his feet. 'An older church 'ere burned in fires set by French pirates, a wicked bunch. See, the floor's black from them ole flames. Pirates 'ave been raidin' Portland for hundreds o' years.'

Isabel followed him to the altar, where a stone marked with a cross was set into the floor of the chancel. She tugged his sleeve.

101

'Flintlock Groves is looking for you. And the pirate, Cutlass. I think both of them want your treasure.'

'I know Flintlock well enough,' said Red Pete. 'Cutlass is a greedy fool. Did ye find me cabin boy?'

Isabel took a deep breath. 'He's planning to take the *Fortune* from you.'

Red Pete laughed ruefully. 'Not alone he won't. He's a slip of a lad, barely seaworthy.' He looked at her sharply. 'Are ye sayin' me ship's back at last?'

A boom of cannon fire shuddered through the church. Isabel snatched at his sleeve, but Red Pete was already lumbering for the church door. The budgie flew behind him, skimming through the heavy door a split second before it slammed. Isabel fumbled with the latch. She flung open the church door.

Ryder stumbled into her. A soaking wet Gregor also greeted her joyfully, jumping up at her with wet paws. 'Me and the dog dude went for a swim over the cliff. Saw a pirate ship. I put the hound over my shoulder and climbed on board to sing some sea shanties. But the pirates were stressed about finding a bloke called Red Roger and threw us overboard,' panted Ryder. 'I guess that's the pirate dude over there with the green budgie.'

Red Pete was standing by a tall chestnut tree. 'The *Fortune*!' he shouted. 'My ship's back at last.'

'Too late,' snarled Cutlass, stepping from the shade of a tree, a sword flashing in his hand.

Penfold Lucke and Mrs Greychurch sat at the kitchen table in Lucke Cottage. Both of them had climbing rope wrapped around their wrists, tying them to the chairs. Mrs Greychurch's face was bright pink, her eyes bulging and her chin wobbling. She had not spoken since the pirates left with various goods, including Penfold's best tea-set.

'Oooomph!' she gasped at last. 'Pirates! How dare they attack me? Here! At the cottage! In broad daylight!'

Penfold tried to free his hands. 'I thought they were quite friendly really. They left a hammock in the garden and answered some questions for my story before they left. They seemed very interested in my pirate book.'

'They tied us to these chairs!' gasped Mrs Greychurch.

'Well, I suppose they have to keep up appearances. They're marauding pirates, after all,' said Penfold calmly. 'Mr Otter even made you a cup of tea.'

'Yes, but I can't drink it!' seethed Mrs Greychurch, wriggling her fingers.

'I need to make some notes for my book. Nice of Hardy to leave us some biscuits too.' He nodded to a pile of chocolate biscuits arranged neatly on a plate. 'I wonder where they found all this climbing rope.' Groover the cat skulked around the chairs. He nibbled the end of the rope.

Mrs Greychurch struggled furiously, working her hands free. 'I'll collect my gunpowder from home. No time to waste.' Within seconds, she was hurtling from the kitchen door. Penfold heard her footsteps heading down the garden path. He shook his hands, still firmly tied to the chair.

Moments later, the door was flung back again with a crash as Mrs Greychurch belted into the kitchen and untied him. 'I thought you'd forgotten me,' gasped Penfold.

'Come with me! This is a pirate emergency. It's time to destroy that ship,' she ordered. She pulled Penfold to his feet and they raced from the cottage to her car. The Volvo roared up Weston Street, leaving a dark plume of exhaust fumes.

'Riaow,' said Groover, annoyed to have been left behind. He jumped on to the kitchen windowsill, knocking off a flower pot, and settled down sulkily for a nap in the sunshine.

'Yo ho ho and a bottle of rum!' shouted Ryder. 'Look out behind you, Red Roger!'

Cutlass swung his sword through the air, missing Red Pete. 'Look at ye, the great pirate captain o' the *Fortune*, no sword by yer side!' he scowled.

Red Pete side-stepped another swipe. 'You're too slow wi' a sword, Cutlass. A snail could evade ye. What've ye done to Tom?'

''Ee listens to me. I've taught 'im all manner o' things,' growled Cutlass.

'I tol' you to look after that boy!'

'I looked after 'im fer 2 years. When he first came aboard an' was sea sick, I sat with 'im. That boy thinks yer naught but a sea dog an' a scoundrel.' He lashed out again and Red Pete jumped over the sword. 'Where's the Spanish treasure?' He swung the sword again and Red Pete stepped lightly out of the way. Cutlass twirled on one heel, bringing the sword around in a circle and missed Red Pete completely. Dizzily, he bounced into a tree.

Red Pete sighed and held up his hand. 'Enough. You're the island's worst swordsman and a pathetic pirate.'

'What treasure?' yelled Ryder. Gregor barked furiously.

'It's not a show,' Isabel shouted at Ryder.

'No one knows the place,' said Red Pete quietly. 'It's dry, well hidden. A cave over yonder. But I know you, Cutlass. Yer lost without a ship and the piratin' life. Once the gold's all spent, you'll be back to sea. Now, where's Tom?'

Cutlass sheathed the sword. 'Headin' this way, I'm sure o' it. He sees a great future for himself as pirate cap'n o' the *Fortune*. He listens to that mermaid ye fear so greatly.'

'What d'ye know o' the Siren? What's she done to Tom?' demanded Red Pete. But Cutlass had already backed away and was running into the woods.

Isabel and Ryder joined Red Pete as he turned to look at the *Fortune*, bobbing gently on the waves in the bay. 'If the mermaid's enchanted Tom, my crew are in grave danger,' he said.

'Wish I'd brought my ukulele,' sighed Ryder. He sat back in the rowing boat and sang loudly as Red Pete and Isabel took an oar each and rowed towards the *Fortune*. 'When I went down to Church Ope Cove, hey ho me hearties,' he warbled. 'Down there I found a treasure trove, with a nilly dilly, hey ho me hearties.'

Gregor raised his black and white nose and howled, 'Waroooh.'

'Dilly me hearties,' squawked the budgie from Red Pete's shoulder.

'You shouldn't have told Cutlass where to look for the treasure,' said Isabel.

''Tis no matter. Keeps 'im out o' the way. I can capture treasure any day o' the week. Cutlass is a greedy ole fool. He grew up here on the Isle. His family are dead 'n' gone now. He's naught but piratin' in his life, and a fair pirate he is too. He'll come to his senses. It takes some men this way. They go maraudin' happy as a fish for years, then all of a sudden the sight of a scrap o' gold makes 'em mad,' replied Red Pete.

'What are you planning to do about Tom Lucke?' asked Isabel.

Red Pete looked uneasy. 'I plan to sail my ship far away from him an' that evil sea witch. I'll head for th' Americas.'

'I don't think you can leave here without him,' warned Isabel, remembering her conversation with Alfie. 'You belong together, the Portland Pirates. And he's just as much a pirate as you are.'

They drifted closer to the *Fortune*, the waves lapping at the small boat. Exhausted, Gregor draped himself across Isabel's knees and nodded off.

'Ahoy everyone!' called Ryder to the ship.

Shorty, leaning over the ship's rail, shouted to the pirates, 'Red Pete's back!'

Red Pete rested the oar. 'Is 'e a good friend o' yours?' he asked, nodding at Ryder.

Isabel winced. 'I s'pose so.'

'D'ye think 'e'll stop singin' with that dog of 'is now? Else I'll 'ave to throw him overboard.'

'No worries, Red Roger, I'll save the shanties for later,' agreed Ryder, scrambling to his feet and eager to climb aboard.

Isabel gasped. She had spotted a small figure climbing the rigging, already half way to the crow's nest. She shook Gregor awake and handed his lead to Ryder. Grabbing the nearest rope, she climbed up the side of the ship, using the cannon ports as footholds. The budgie flew up ahead of her. 'Suzie, get down from there!' she yelled.

'I'm a pirate!' Suzie called down, clinging on to a rope. With a sigh she started to climb down.

Ben appeared from the hold with a chisel and looked up at Suzie sheepishly. 'I told her not to go up the rigging again. I'm just helping to adjust the ship's compass. I've got a navigation app on my iPhone. Here, let me show you,' he said to Bill.

'Fair enough,' said Bill.

Ben flicked the iPhone on and took the pirate through his latest app. 'And that's how I work out exactly where we are, using a satellite in the sky,' he ended.

'Ah,' said Bill, looking up at the sky. 'Like the moon 'n' stars.'

Ryder clambered over the side of the boat, his face bright red, with Gregor over his shoulder. He dropped the dog onto the deck and Gregor bounded to greet Suzie, jumping up at the rigging.

'I'll show Gregor where the food's kept. I think Mr Otter'll like him,' said Suzie, scrambling down the rigging. 'Gregor loves biscuits.' She took his lead.

'I'll come with you,' said Ryder. 'Is there any food aboard? I'm starving. Gregor ate all the cakes before we ran into Red Roger and I need some lunch.' They disappeared into the cabins below deck.

'All hands make sail!' roared Red Pete. 'I'll not linger by this enchanted Isle another minute!'

Hardy, Bleet and Shorty ran to raise the sails, turning the capstans. Red Pete took the helm.

'Where are we going?' shouted Isabel.

'We'll cut south along the coast, sail the channel 'twixt the *Race* an' the shore. I want to be far away from them gallows where they hang pirates in Waymuthe, an' out o' sight o' that schemin' Siren by nightfall,' called Red Pete.

Ben tapped Isabel on the shoulder. 'I'm guessing this is some sort of pirate game,' he said, more calmly than she had expected. 'Nothing whatsoever to do with time travel, dragons or any of that nonsense.'

'I'll explain later,' said Isabel.

CHAPTER NINETEEN
PIRATE ATTACK

Penfold Lucke, Miranda and Mrs Greychurch arrived at Cheyne Weares with the cannon in the back of Mrs Greychurch's Volvo estate. 'Help me unload it,' she shouted, leaping from the car. 'At last, we can get rid of all those pirates in one shot!'

'Mother, isn't it illegal to fire a cannon?' asked Miranda.

Mrs Greychurch gripped her by the shoulders, the wind blowing her hair wildly around her face. 'One day you'll understand! I'm doing this to free Portland from the tyranny of pirates.'

'Tyranny of pirates,' repeated Penfold, writing in his notebook. 'Excellent. I'll use that for my first chapter.'

They set up the cannon, overlooking the sweeping seas to the east of the Isle, and waited. As dusk fell, a school of silvery dolphins leaped in the water, heading towards the Bill. Swallows swooped around the shore, the last rays of sun catching their red and blue flashes. Then Penfold pointed across the sea. 'There she is!' he shouted gleefully. The *Fortune* sailed into view.

'Ready? Fire!' cried Mrs Greychurch. Miranda lit the fuse on the cannon and it fizzled and faded. Nonetheless, the ground beneath them shuddered as if a small earthquake shook the island.

'Whassat?' gasped Miranda, clinging to the sturdy cannon as the land shook. Rocks tumbled from the fissured cliffs below them.

'It's like footsteps,' said Mrs Greychurch.

'Thunder,' corrected Penfold, scribbling notes. He sat on the cannon. 'Don't shoot at the ship yet. You'll frighten them off. How many cannon do you think the ship has? Is that a mermaid figurehead? I'm so pleased I've found the *Fortune* before that cunning girl, Isabel Maydew. She wants to beat me to the story. But my *Portland Pirates* will be fantastic. There'll be a fiendish pirate captain, a mutinous cabin boy and a crocodile.'

'I think that's called *Peter Pan*,' said Miranda, crossing her arms.

On board the *Fortune*, Ben was busy showing his iPhone recipe app to Mr Otter. Isabel made her way past Hardy and Bleet, working on deck. A sharp gust of wind caught the sails. Looking ahead, Isabel saw the Portland *Race* churning into huge white-topped waves. Tall slender water spouts twisted from the sea and lightning flashed in sudden zigzags.

'You can't leave without Tom Lucke! You won't be able to sail the *Fortune* through there,' she shouted at Red Pete.

The captain held the ship's wheel tightly, as thunder crackled around them. 'The mermaid's behind this, I know it!' Suddenly he froze, looking over Isabel's shoulder. She followed his gaze. Tom was standing behind her, still as a church statue, holding a glittering sword.

Red Pete spoke quietly to him. 'I searched for ye day an' night.' The wind ran through his red hair, blowing it across his face. 'Cutlass an' the mermaid told ye lies, Tom.'

'Cutlass taught me how to fix up a boat, an' handle a sword,' said Tom coldly. He stepped closer to Red Pete and raised the sword as the silent crew approached, the only sound the ripple of wind in the sails. 'When I fell into the sea, none of ye feared I was lost. If t'weren't fer the mermaid, I'd 'ave drowned. All you cared for was yer gold an' silver!'

'We've no need for jewels, just our ship,' said Red Pete.

'This will be *my* ship,' said Tom.

There was a scuffle from the foredeck. 'Here's yer treasure!' Flintlock climbed from the hold with a heavy sack, pushing past Bleet.

Cutlass stumbled after him. 'Flintlock found the cave afore me. Took me gold, the varmint.'

The smuggler flung the sack across the deck, sending goblets, chains and gold coins spinning. Turning on his heel, he unsheathed his sword and threw it to Red Pete. 'Take my weapon. Not as fine as Tom's fancy silver sword, but the blade's sharp enough.'

'It's not his sword!' shouted Red Pete, jumping to catch Flintlock's blade. ''Tis mine, just as the *Fortune*'s mine. Ye'll not take 'er from me, Tom.'

The pirate captain faced the cabin boy. Tom gritted his teeth. He gripped the heavy sword in both hands. Sunlight glinted on the silver blade. The pirates parted, creating a circle on the deck around Red Pete and Tom. The captain stepped forward, raising the sword and striking at Tom. The blade missed him by a finger breadth. Tom deflected a second strike. Red Pete frowned, twirling the sword in his hand.

Backing a few steps away, almost to the side of the ship, Tom set his feet firmly and swung the blade, meeting Red Pete's sword with a ringing clang. In a few blows, Tom backed Red Pete to the ship's wheel. The captain twisted away, slicing Tom's sleeve. The boy stepped back, out of breath. His sword hung heavily from his hands, the point of the blade resting on the deck.

'Let him go!' shouted Isabel. Hardy caught her by the arm, pulling her away from Tom. As Red Pete advanced on Tom, the boy suddenly stood upright. Wrenching the sword upwards, he flicked away Red Pete's weapon, sending it spinning towards the treasure across the deck. Moving quickly, he pinned Red Pete to the main mast, with the sword poised over his throat.

'Let's not be hasty,' said Red Pete, raising his hands.

'Fine piece of swordsmanship, young Tom,' called Shorty.

The other pirates murmured agreement, 'Not bad.'

''Specially since that ole fool Cutlass taught 'im,' said Hardy.

Bleet nodded, 'Cutlass wields a sword like a lady eatin' sweetmeats.'

'I showed 'im all them moves!' snapped Cutlass.

Flintlock edged towards the cabin boy. 'Tread lightly, young Tom. Ye'll not harm yer captain.'

'What's a Groves doin' aboard my ship anyhow?' asked Red Pete, swivelling his eyes to Flintlock, while Tom pressed the blade to his throat.

'I've been keeping an eye out for the *Fortune*. I wished to make amends. I never 'ad time to say I was wrong to mock ye all those years ago. P'raps a Siren did sing to ye and tell tales o' the sea. An' ye left the Isle so sudden.' He pointed at the boy. 'Why did ye take Tom to sea?'

'T'was no life for the boy ashore,' said Red Pete, looking directly at Tom. 'He's a Lucke. The mermaid was seekin' him out. With me escapin' her clutches, she had her emerald eyes set on him as her prize.'

'Better to swim with a mermaid than slave on the *Fortune* fer you,' snarled Tom.

Red Pete raised his hand to the blade at his throat. 'Ye learned how to handle the sea and a sword on my ship. I know the Siren too well, Tom. She watches the Luckes closely. If ye take my ship wi' that sword she gave thee, she'll 'ave a hold upon ye forever.'

Tom kept his grip on the sword, but Isabel could see that he was unsure. He frowned, his hands trembling. Isabel looked from the boy to the captain. Although Tom was thin and wiry, the two were alike, Tom's hair almost as fiery as Red Pete's.

'Your real name's Peter Lucke, isn't it?' she said slowly.

Red Pete nodded.

'Lucke?' gasped Tom. He wiped one of his shaking hands on his shirt.

'He's your brother,' said Isabel.

Tom's face paled. 'My brother went to work for a Portsmouth merchant 10 years ago.'

'True,' agreed Red Pete, 'I learned the routes that merchant boats took and where to pick up a fine ship for piratin'.'

Tom turned to Isabel and grabbed her sleeve. 'Is this true? When I tol' Mrs Groves my story, she told me to trust *you*, not the mermaid. I thought you were a stowaway that night i' the storm, then a witch with fiendish powers. I wandered the Isle for days, followin' you from west to east.'

Isabel nodded. 'The mermaid sent the storm to lure both you and Red Pete back to the shores of Portland. Here she has some power over you and your fate. I've been trying to help you.'

Tom looked from Isabel to Red Pete. Finally, he flung away the sword.

''Bout time the boy knew the truth,' said Hardy.

Red Pete dusted down his coat and wiped his forehead on his sleeve. He looked around him at the crew. 'I'd no need to defeat the lad. Best to let 'im win an' say his piece.'

Suddenly a cannon ball whistled overhead and exploded into the ship. Fire ripped along the edge of the boat towards the mermaid figurehead, sending a plume of flames into the sky. The lower sails ignited and the fire roared as the growing breeze fanned the flames.

'The ship's on fire!' cried Mrs Greychurch. Miranda had her fingers stuffed in her ears. 'Load up some more gunpowder, Miranda,' she ordered. 'We can fire again.'

'Ouch, that was loud,' said Penfold.

'Aachoo!' sneezed Miranda, blowing the rest of the gunpowder into a cloud.

Mrs Greychurch sat on the cannon. 'I don't believe it,' she said, 'that's all our gunpowder gone.'

Mrs Groves arrived in the Land Rover and squeezed into Cheyne Weares car park. 'Has anyone seen Gregor?' she called, leaning out of the window. 'Ryder took him out for a walk and they're late. It's Gregor's tea time. Oh dear, that ship looks in trouble.'

Hardy, Shorty and Bill formed a chain and passed buckets of water hand to hand to put out the flames. Smoke billowed across the deck. Cutlass pointed accusingly at Flintlock. ''Tis the smuggler's fault. Ee stole our treasure, an' now the Revenue men are on our tail blastin' us to bits,' he said, throwing water over the flames.

Flintlock pointed at the gloomy shore. 'That's no Revenue man. She's wearin' a pink scarf.'

'Ah, Veronica Greychurch. More fearsome than ole King Henry and 'is oyster-shaped fort in Castletown,' remarked Red Pete. 'She'd make a fine pirate. Thankfully, it seems she's run out o' firepower.' Even from a distance, they could hear a squawk of raised voices.

Isabel rubbed her face, black with soot, her arms and hands burning from the heat of the fire. She threw another pail of water. The flames on the bow were fizzling out and black smoke drifted in a plume into the sky.

'The mermaid's burned to a cinder,' shuddered Tom. He scooped up some of the coins, goblets and chains still scattered around the deck and turned to Red Pete. 'What will we do with all this treasure?'

Red Pete leaned on the side of the ship and stared towards Portland. Finally he said, 'Remember the holes i' the walls of Dovecote cottage, where ole Mrs Quarry lives? I want them fixed an' she should 'ave a fire burnin' in the hearth next winter. The Southwell fishermen need new fishin' nets an' a bigger boat.'

Flintlock picked up a coin and tossed it in the air. He looked at Red Pete. 'We'll make a deal. Leave the finest jewels for those in need. An' I'll make sure them that needs help gets it. Ye can put me ashore over yonder near Freshwater Bay. I've no hankerin' to sail the Southern seas. I want to see my ole farm again.'

'Pfff, we're meant to be pirates, not ladies o' charity. Soon we'll all be sittin' here doin' needlepoint, drinkin' tea from china pots and chattin' about sermons,' sniffed Cutlass.

'All of you know what it is to be poor,' Red Pete jabbed his finger at the crew and they nodded silently.

'What about my family?' called Bill.

'They'll have fat chickens runnin' in the yard,' promised Flintlock.

'Waste o' decent gold!' snapped Cutlass. He pulled out a saw and began repair work to the ship. 'Looks like I'm stuck wi' bein' a pirate, to keep Bill's chickens fed on Portland.'

'The gold's mine,' squawked the budgie, landing on Red Pete's shoulder.

Red Pete leaned against the mast and folded his arms. He looked long and hard at Tom. 'What shall I do with ee?'

Tom's mouth was set in a line. 'I'm not going back to Weston. I belong at sea.'

He glanced quickly at Isabel and she stepped forward. 'You owe him another chance. Tom's worked hard for you. You didn't tell him he was your brother. One day, Tom'll be a great pirate too.'

'The witch is right, he *is* a true pirate, keen with a sword,' commented Shorty. He patted Tom on the back. 'And ee's a good cabin lad, yet we paid 'im little due.'

'No doubt,' said Red Pete. He sniffed and rubbed his nose. Finally he relented. 'I'll watch him like a hawk from now on. Any more signs o' mutiny and I'll throw 'im overboard to that fiendish mermaid.' He scooped up his sword and twirled it lightly in his hand. 'You'll need to work hard to make amends, both you an' Cutlass.'

Cutlass muttered under his breath, 'Thought ee was better off on land.'

Red Pete continued, 'Tom, you can work with Shorty 'n' Bill.' He turned to Isabel. 'Are you an' your friends sailin' with us? That tall boy with the compass may be handy and the girl can climb the crow's nest. Not sure about yer singing dog and 'is friend with breeches like blue sails.'

Isabel looked at the dark cliffs of Portland. Night was drawing in. On the sea, silver lights flickered as shoals of fish swam alongside the ship. She wondered what would happen if they sailed with the *Fortune*, what amazing things they would see.

Suzie and Gregor appeared from the cabin below deck. She tugged Isabel's sleeve. 'Why are you so sooty? We have to go home.

It's your birthday tomorrow and I need to count out 13 candles for your cake.'

'I've got cakes in boxes a'plenty fer you, Tom, from that big hall o' food on land,' noted Mr Otter. 'It's yer birthday tomorrow as well. I've got tallow candles but I'm not ruinin' a cake with 'em.'

Gregor jumped up at the side of the ship, gazing wistfully at the shore.

'Gregor!' a thin voice shrieked from the cliffs.

Isabel looked towards the land again, where Mrs Groves was waving frantically at them. Her mother would be finishing the birthday cake and later Suzie would fix the candles in a wonky circle. 'Call Ben and Ryder from the galley. We have to go home,' she said.

She turned to Tom. 'Are you sure you want to stay on the *Fortune*?'

Tom smiled, 'It's where I belong.'

Red Pete took the helm. 'I'll sail in near the shore. Give my good wishes to that fine lady, Veronica Greychurch, who's lurkin' by 'er cannon. An' please take all yer friends with you.'

CHAPTER TWENTY

A BIRTHDAY CAKE

Mrs Groves clutched Penfold's arm. 'Gregor's on board that ship! What are we going to do?' She ran to the edge of the cliffs, waving frantically. 'You'll have to swim out and rescue him.'

The ground trembled. It felt as if heavy footsteps were drawing closer. Miranda and Mrs Greychurch turned slowly. They saw a dark shadow silhouetted against the sky.

'It's the giant!' gasped Miranda. The figure faded into the wind like a cloud scattered by the breeze. They turned back to the ship. Catching the tide, the *Fortune* was heading south. The first stars of the evening appeared low in the sky.

While Tom took the helm, Red Pete stood at the bow of the ship, staring into the water as if he were looking for someone. When the mermaid emerged from the sea, he raised his arm in farewell to her. Finally, she splashed her tail, sending a cascade of water into the air. In the same moment, the tall masts glittered and the ship sparkled with a silvery light. Then just an outline remained and the *Fortune* vanished into the sea, like a ghost. The mermaid disappeared beneath the water.

'The ship's gone again!' shouted Penfold, flinging down his notebook in disgust. 'How am I supposed to write this book if I can't talk to the pirate captain? I'll have to make up the story and that could take weeks!'

'You'd better start writing then,' snapped Mrs Greychurch, folding her arms and tapping her toe.

'What about Gregor?' cried Mrs Groves. 'He's disappeared on a ghost ship. They won't have any of his special dog biscuits. It upsets his tummy when he goes sailing.'

'Look, there's Isabel. I've been looking for her. She's always sneaking off,' shouted Miranda.

Isabel, Ryder, Ben and Suzie were running across the narrow beach near Freshwater Bay, with Gregor bounding ahead. Ben and Isabel were arguing. 'Of course we weren't in the 17th century. It was a pirate *theme* ship,' said Ben.

'We travelled across time,' insisted Isabel. 'Red Pete's a real pirate. Just now, that roar of thunder was a time shift. We returned to the present day.'

'Rubbish,' said Ben. 'It was cannon fire.'

Suzie was warbling, 'Happy birthday to yoooo, squashed potatoes and glue.'

'Warooh!' howled Gregor.

'Ahoy and a bottle of rum, we've been on a pirate day trip! Ate loads of ship's biscuits!' shouted Ryder, waving up at Mrs Groves. 'Have you seen my board? I left it around the bay somewhere. Hope the mer-babe hasn't taken it again. Perfect weather for windsurfing. Slow down, dog dude!'

Gregor flew up the path like a black and white rocket and jumped into Mrs Groves' arms.

Mrs Maydew carried the enormous birthday cake into the kitchen. All 13 candles were alight and Isabel could see their reflections in Suzie's wide blue eyes. Suzie sat with her elbows on the table, a fork already in her hand.

'Happy birthday to you,' sang Alfie and Peggy. Ryder was strumming his ukulele, a wet surfboard propped against the wall behind him. The two cats, Surfer and Nellie, watched the cake with interest, licking their paws. Gregor had his paws up on the table and was panting as close to the cake as he could get.

'What d'you think?' asked Mrs Maydew.

'I wasn't expecting a pirate ship,' admitted Isabel. The cake had chocolate icing around the bow, blue icing for the sea and little squishy marshmallow figures on board. An iced mermaid reclined on a rock. There was even a black liquorice flag.

'I sailed on a real pirate ship yesterday,' said Suzie, her tricorn hat crammed over her ears.

'I don't think Mrs Greychurch would approve of a pirate cake,' noted Mrs Groves. 'She's dismantling her cannon, after "vanquishing the pirate menace". That's what she said, anyway. There was a nasty incident at Mr Lucke's cottage with pirates and climbing rope.'

She looked sideways at Alfie and he shuffled his feet. 'Get down, Gregor! Oh dear, I am sorry. Look, he's only licked one side of the cake.'

'Treasure 'n' lace, brandy 'n' gold,' hummed Ryder, strumming the ukulele.

'Still, I hear Penfold is writing his pirate story. He says he's going to include Isabel, Suzie, Ben and even Gregor in the adventure,' added Mrs Groves.

Isabel blew out the candles and sat at the kitchen table with Suzie to eat her cake. While everyone joined in with another pirate sea shanty, she gazed out of the window towards Deadman's Bay, where the sheer west cliffs dropped to the sea. She thought about Tom Lucke, who somewhere, far across the seas of time, would also be celebrating his birthday. And she remembered what the mermaid had said to Suzie, about a sleeping giant. She ate a forkful of cake. She would always wonder where they sailed next and what happened when Tom Lucke finally became captain of the *Fortune*.

Pirate Captain Tom Lucke strode along the foot of the West Cliffs, a curved sword strapped to his belt over a white silk shirt, a black tricorn low on his forehead. The *Fortune* was anchored nearby. By Thunderbolts Hole he heard a distant roll of thunder that boomed and echoed along the cliffs and through the caves. He saw a shimmer of turquoise tail and felt cold green eyes following him. As he suspected, the beautiful but sinister mermaid was waiting for him, perched on dark, sloping Blacknor Rock. He jumped from rock to rock until he reached Blacknor, where the waves lapped gently as the tide ebbed.

'Sso you returned to the *Fortune* to sserve your foolish brother, Red Pete. I told you to use the ssword and your witss and take the ship,' sighed the mermaid.

'I regret nothing, mermaid. I served Red Pete well for many years after that,' said Tom.

The mermaid splashed her tail impatiently. 'What hass become of your fine captain now?'

'We sailed the *Fortune* to the Americas where we met a man called John Wesley stranded by a storm, his ship's mast broken almost in two. After talking for many days with him, Pete cut his hair and took a Bible ashore to save souls. He came back to Portland and built a chapel o' yonder in Weston.' He jabbed a finger at the mermaid. 'You gave me my own brother's sword, set with rubies and silver.'

The mermaid shrugged her pale shoulders. 'Yes, but I ssaved your life. You sshould be grateful to me, Portland pirate.'

Tom rubbed his fiery beard. 'I am. I had a new figurehead carved for the *Fortune* to honour you. Sirens don't see things as people do. It's my birthday today, same day as Isabel. I always remember her on this day. She spoke up for me, tol' my brother an' the crew to treat me better. She said I would be a great pirate.' He glanced towards the distant cottages at the top of the cliffs.

The mermaid hissed angrily, 'You should forget her. Isabel tried to desstroy the Isle of Portland after the *Fortune* left. She woke up the island giant.'

Tom sat down on the rock next to the mermaid, his buckled boots scraping the surface. 'Tell me what happened,' he said.

'It began as the autumn nights were drawing in, dark as a velvet cape,' said the mermaid. Flipping her tail in the water and twirling her long red hair, she began to tell Tom the story of Isabel Maydew and the Portland Giant.

About *Portland Pirates*

What is a pirate?

A pirate is someone who attacks and robs ships or coastal towns. The seafaring coast of Dorset has a long history of piracy and smuggling.

Were there real Portland pirates?

Pirates have been attracted to Portland for hundreds of years. A Saxon called Portus may even have given his name to the island. He pirated the south coast of England, landing on the Isle around 703 AD. In a Saxon Charter of King Ethelred, the island's name was recorded as Portelond.

In 789, three Viking ships landed at Church Ope. The King's Reeve or sheriff, Beaduheard, rode from Dorchester to greet them. The Vikings killed him and his companions, setting the scene for the ransack of other places along the British coast. *Ransack* is a Viking word, one of many still in use today. *Ope,* meaning *opening* to the sea, may also have Viking origins.

French pirates attacked Portland during the Hundred Years War, destroying the first St Andrew's Church at Church Ope. Around this time, King Edward III told English pirates to attack all French shipping. Local pirates happily complied, and attacked all other foreign ships as well!

By the Elizabethan era, many pirate ships were lurking off the coast of Dorset. In 1580, a proclamation declared that Dorset pirates 'at this day commit more spoils and robberies on all sides than have been heard of in former times'.

Are there pirate graves on Portland?

The so-called pirate graves may be found in the churchyard of ruined St Andrew's Church, marked with skull and crossbones. Some people believe these graves belonged to wealthy local stonemasons rather than pirates. The skull and crossbones was a mediaeval symbol for death.

Is Captain Red Pete based on a local pirate?

The character of Captain Red Pete was inspired by stories about local pirates. *Harry Paye*, the Poole pirate, captured French and Spanish ships and took prisoners for ransom. He sailed from an island in Poole Harbour, where he buried his treasure. In 1405, the French and Spanish sailed five galleys and two smaller ships with crossbowmen into Poole Harbour in revenge against Harry. In a fierce battle, the people of Poole drove back the invaders. Two years later, with 15 ships at his command, Harry captured 120 French vessels and brought them back to Poole.

Henry Strangways, born in Dorset to a well-known family, was known as a Gentleman Pirate. He used Portland Castle as a pirate den to store his loot. In 1555 he was imprisoned in the Tower of London. After his death he received a Royal Pardon from Queen Elizabeth I.

Sir Walter Raleigh, a soldier, explorer and Elizabethan pirate, was made Captain of Portland Castle in 1592. From here, he had drawn up plans to defeat the mighty Spanish Armada in 1588. A ferocious battle had taken place just off Portland in July 1588, with many local boats ferrying men and supplies of ammunition to the English fleet, including a number of local privateers.

Do the pirate crew from the Fortune talk like real pirates?

The pirates' speech includes some old Dorset dialect. Real pirates' language was *very* colourful; their speech would have included French, Spanish and Dutch slang picked up on the trade routes.

Why is the pirate ship called the Fortune?

I named Red Pete's ship after the *Fortune*, a pilgrim ship that sailed to the Americas in 1621 with 35 settlers. The *Fortune* was captured and plundered by French pirates on its return voyage. Another ship called the *Royal Fortune* was captured by a pirate called Black Bart.

How did you find out about sailing a pirate ship?

I talked to Andy Straw, a tug-boat skipper based at Portland Port, about capstans, anchors and rigging. I also looked around the *TS Pelican* in Weymouth Harbour. *TS Pelican* was converted to a tall ship in 2007 and its sail plan was based on a Barbary Coast (North African) pirate ship.

Why is there a mermaid figurehead on the **Fortune**?

In 2008, a carving of a mermaid was recovered from the bow of the Swash Channel Wreck, a 17th-century merchant ship lying just outside Poole Harbour. The wreck also inspired my description of the *Fortune's* cargo. Iron cannons, barrels, pewter and musket balls were found in the wreckage.

How did you research rock climbing for **Portland Pirates**?

Rich from *New Heights Climbing* helped with this. I tried out a harness and climbing shoes, as well as ropes and clips used for climbing. There are nearly 900 climbing routes on Portland. Many have weird names, such as *Yikes Shaggy! Reptile Smile* and *Hall of Mirrors*. Climbing is another unique facet of Portland, which brings people to the Isle from all over the world.

Thanks to Professor Anne Morriss, friend and fellow author, for checking my pirate research.

ABOUT THE AUTHOR

Carol is the author of *The Portland Sea Dragon* and *Enchantment of the Black Dog*, the first two books in *The Portland Chronicles* series. Her stories draw on local folklore, myth and legend, such as Veasta, the Chesil Beach sea monster, and the Roy Dog, the phantom Portland Black Dog. Her writing is inspired by the magic and mystery of the Isle. Carol has three children and lives in Easton, Portland. She studied English Literature and History at university and has worked with young people as an adviser. Since the publication of her books, she has given talks in schools and libraries across Dorset. In her free time, she loves to read stories about pirates and sing sea shanties.

You can keep up to date with Carol by following her blog at
http://carolhunt.blogspot.com/.

For the latest news, events and photographs look on Facebook at
The Portland Sea Dragon.

You can also follow **islandseadragon** on Twitter.

Have you read Books 1 and 2
of THE PORTLAND CHRONICLES?

'Adventures inspired by the sea ... Drawing on local history, *The Portland Chronicles* explore a seventeenth-century world of smuggling, witchcraft, piracy and intrigue.'

(*View From Weymouth and Portland*)

'*The Portland Sea Dragon* is an enchanting tale set in the near future. When the dragon is accused of the murder of Sally Lucke in 1616, only Isabel in 2011 can solve the mystery. So she sets out on a time-travelling adventure.'

(*Free Portland News*, March 2010)

'*The Portland Sea Dragon*, which is Carol's first book, is an all-Dorset production, with the book's artwork by Poole-based artist Domini Deane and published by husband and wife team Tim and Julie Musk of Dorchester-based *Roving Press*.'

(*Blackmore Vale Magazine*, 16 April 2010)

'A mum-of-three has achieved her dream of writing a children's book after being inspired by the legends of Portland ... *The Portland Sea Dragon* ... follows 12-year-old Isabel whose curiosity about the past draws her back to 1616 where she encounters an island witch and solves the mystery of a young woman's disappearance.'

(*Dorset Echo*, 27 February 2010)

'Heroes, villains and bedtime stories for all ... To assist the children with their story writing, they learnt about what it takes to be the hero or the villain, naughty or nice, good guy or bad guy. Special guest for the evening was author Carol Hunt who read extracts from her new book *The Portland Sea Dragon* ably assisted by two lovely puppets.'

(*View From Weymouth and Portland*, 17 March 2010)

'In *Enchantment of the Black Dog*, Isabel Maydew unravels the legend of the phantom Black Dog of Portland. Her adventures include Ryder, a local windsurfer, a sinister mermaid and the Southwell fairy. Isabel travels across time to the Ice Ages and English Civil War to solve the mystery, with the story culminating at Portland Castle, where a ghostly black dog has indeed been seen.'

(*View from Weymouth and Portland*,
24 November 2010)

'If the first book *The Portland Sea Dragon* is anything to go by, *Enchantment of the Black Dog* is a must for all ages. I found it an exciting read and look forward to reading Carol's latest.'

(*Free Portland News*, January 2011)

'Both these popular children's books have far outsold everything else, making Carol the outright winner ... Books 1 and 2 have flown off the shelves of bookshops, since Carol's amazing imagination first conjured up a world of magical dragons, mermaids and time travel, interwoven with local folklore.'

(Imagine Books, Weymouth)

About the Illustrator

Domini Deane is a self-taught artist, who has been creating magical worlds and creatures since she could pick up a crayon. Born in the Rocky Mountains of Colorado, she now lives and works in Dorset, England. Her favourite medium is watercolour with a pinch of fairy dust, and her greatest inspiration is a blank piece of paper. For more information visit www.dominideane.com.

'Young up-and-coming painter and illustrator Domini Deane paints fantastical watercolours and at 26 has just been published for the first time. Domini is like a Pre-Raphaelite painting come to life, with her long auburn tresses and porcelain complexion – a perfect blend to complement her style of watercolour painting, which she has had an all-consuming passion for since she was old enough to hold a paintbrush.'

(*Western Gazette*, 26 March 2010)

'Illustrator Domini Deane, whose artwork brings the mythical world to life, was also signing books and helping eager youngsters with their drawing' [at the launch of *The Portland Sea Dragon*].

(*View From Weymouth and Portland*, 7 April 2010).

'This was also the first book commission for Poole-based artist and illustrator Domini Deane, who provided the artwork for the book, capturing the mood and setting of the story in extraordinary detail.'

(*thisisdorset.co.uk*, 14 April 2010)

OTHER ROVING PRESS TITLES

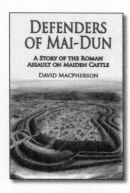

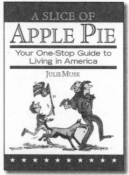